I0578714

WILD AND FREE

HONEYWELLS OF KENTUCKY, BOOK 5

VANESSA GRAY BARTAL

DRY CREEK PRESS

Copyright © 2012, 2021 by Vanessa Gray Bartal

This is a work of fiction. Names, characters, places, and incidents either are the product of the author's imagination or are used fictitiously. Any resemblance to actual persons, living or dead, events, or locales is entirely coincidental.

❀ Created with Vellum

Vaughn Drake adjusted her cheerleading skirt, hoping no one would notice. It was unusual for a cheerleader to want to fade into the background, but that was how she felt. She cheered because it was what popular girls did, and Vaughn longed to be popular. And she was popular in her way. Smart, funny, and friendly, she was well-liked by most people. But she longed to be popular in the way all the tiny girls around her were popular, just by merit of being thin, pretty, and blond.

Some people had told Vaughn she was pretty or, rather, that she had a pretty face, not realizing the vast and hurtful distinction between the two phrases. One was a compliment; the other was a well-disguised way of saying she was fat. The worst part was that she couldn't disagree with the assessment. She did have a pretty face. And even though her hair wasn't blond, it was a pretty shade of chestnut brown, long, thick, and well-behaved. That left only the problem of her body, and it was a huge problem. She had tried every diet in the world, but they hadn't worked. She exercised every day, running and lifting weights like a fiend. But there was nothing she could do about her too-tall height or large bones. Behind her back, people called her the Amazon. They did it laughingly, either not guessing or not caring how much the description hurt Vaughn.

The originator of the dreaded nickname jumped down from the stands and began heading her way. Vaughn knew because the crowd started cheering wildly as they did every week when Grant Honeywell decided the cheerleaders needed his special brand of help. She held her breath, praying silently that he would pass by her unnoticed and, miracle of miracles, he did. He sauntered until he reached the center of the crowd and then he begin to do back handsprings, end over end over end like a trained gymnast and not like someone who was 6'8". When he was finished going backwards, he reversed direction and began flipping forward, and the crowd cheered like it was viewing Cirque du Soleil.

Vaughn rolled her eyes, refusing to be impressed. She and Grant had shared a love/hate relationship since the first grade when they were the two tallest kids and class and therefore chosen to be team leaders of kickball. Grant had taken the opponent angle seriously, seemingly never losing sight of Vaughn as a rival. He tormented her on an almost daily basis. Giving her the dreaded nickname was only one of his tactics. Public humiliation was another.

The problem, Vaughn realized as she watched him jump in the air, touch his toes, and land in the splits, was that she was as attracted to Grant as much as any of the other stupid sheep females she knew. How could she help it? He was beautiful and, when he wasn't torturing her, he was fun. And he was nice, at least to other people. He was at every party, but he didn't drink, somehow remaining cool and fun without imbibing in alcohol. Girls fawned over him, but he never dated. The rumor was that he had a long-distance girlfriend, but no one had ever met her. Vaughn didn't want to be attracted to him, though. She wanted to hate him for the awful things he did to her. But whenever she tried, he would do something charming to make her forget. Most of the time, he simply made her nervous.

She was nervous now as he stalked toward her like a panther intent on its prey. She shook her head and backed up, but protesting was futile. What Grant wanted, he got, and today he wanted her for whatever nefarious purpose.

"C'mon, Vaughn," he said, grabbing her hand.

"No," she said, trying to snatch her hand away. "Pick someone else."

"Can't. It has to be you."

"Why?" she asked, tugging desperately at her hand.

"Because you're the only one big enough to do it."

She was pretty sure she hated him then. "What are you doing?" she asked as he positioned her in front of the center of the bleachers.

"I'm going to flip you," he said, lining up behind her and linking their elbows.

"I don't want to be flipped," she said, panicking now. "I'll flip you."

He laughed. "You can't flip me."

"Sure I can," she said. "Shut up and I'll prove it, and then you have to let me go."

"We'll see," he said cryptically.

Vaughn bent over, bracing her feet and pulling Grant's arms so he flipped over her back. She tried to let go of his arms then, but he wouldn't release, pulling her with him as he began to straighten so she leapfrogged over him, rolling over his back so that her cheerleading skirt flipped upside down, revealing the thing she had tried to keep hidden all night. Once on solid ground, she ripped her arms away from him and shook herself free of his clutch.

"What's that?" Grant asked, lifting her skirt for a closer inspection.

"Grant!" Vaughn snapped, ripping her skirt out of his fingers and smoothing it down. It was too late, though. Everyone had seen Vaughn's girdle, the one she had to wear in order to zip her skirt. They were laughing and pointing at her. Vaughn wished for a hole, something large enough to swallow her and provide immediate escape.

Grant's head swiveled between her and the crowd, a stupid smile on his too-handsome face. "Why are they laughing?" he asked.

"As if you don't know," Vaughn said, her voice tremulous with the tears that were pricking her eyes and closing her throat. "Sometimes I really hate you, Grant," she added before turning to run off the field, the sound of laughter echoing loudly behind her.

She ran to the locker room and changed into her regular clothes. She would have gone straight home, but it was an away game, and she needed to ride the bus. So she went into the bathroom stall and waited for her teammates to arrive and change, hoping to slip out of the bathroom unnoticed. It was a vain hope.

"Oh, Vaughn, that was awful," Stacy said. Stacy was one of those girls Vaughn wasn't sure about. Sometimes her kindness seemed sincere, and other times it seemed fake.

"It really was," Danica added. Danica was one of those girls Vaughn was sure she couldn't trust. Come to think of it, she didn't have many true friends on the cheerleading squad. Or in the whole school, for that matter. She liked to think of herself as a lone wolf, but she suspected she was simply a freak. "I can't believe you wore a girdle under your uniform. What were you thinking?"

"She was thinking she's always at the bottom of the pyramid and never gets tossed in the air," Joyce said, snickering behind her hand.

"Stop it," Stacy said. "Y'all are just being mean. Vaughn's been through enough tonight." Facing Vaughn again, she gave her a sympathetic smile. "I can't believe Grant did that to you. That was just cruel."

Vaughn was surprised by the statement; it was no secret that Stacy had a huge crush on Grant and had for years. "Maybe he didn't know," Vaughn said, giving him the benefit of the doubt for once. Grant was typically clueless, and she wasn't able to forget the way he'd asked her why everyone was laughing.

"Of course he knew," Danica said. "Why do you think he did it? His intent was to show everyone your girdle."

"I don't think that's true," Vaughn snapped. The fact that she was actually having to defend Grant now made her even angrier. "Grant's not the brightest bulb in the shed; I'm sure he didn't know what he was doing."

Danica rolled her eyes. "Please, Vaughn, Grant's our salutatorian, and you're trying to say he's stupid?"

"There are different kinds of smart," Vaughn said.

"I think Vaughn has a little crush on Grant," Danica said, her voice oozing pity.

"I do not," Vaughn argued. "I don't even like him."

"Sure," Danica said, checking her perfect face in a tiny little mirror.

"Leave Vaughn alone," Stacy reiterated. "Just forget about it, Vaughn. I'm sure hardly anybody noticed, and even if they did, they'll forget it soon. Are you going to the party tonight?"

Vaughn shook her head. She simply wanted to go home and find release for her pent-up emotions.

"Are you kidding?" Danica said. "She's got a hot date with Ben and Jerry."

"At least I have a date," Vaughn snapped. "Heard from Curtis lately, Danica?" Everyone sucked in a surprised breath. Vaughn was usually sweet and even tempered, or so everyone thought. If people knew how often what she thought was different than what she said, they would be surprised.

"That was mean," Danica said, her pretty blue eyes welling with tears.

"Yeah, it was," Vaughn agreed. "It doesn't feel great when someone walks all over your feelings, does it? Yet you've been doing it to me since the eighth grade, and I'm sick of it. Keep your snide remarks to yourself, or I'll start spilling your secrets. And I don't think you want that, Danica, because I know them all." She turned and stormed away then, feeling empowered as she marched to the bus. Maybe it was time Vaughn developed a backbone because she was getting sincerely tired of being everyone's doormat.

She expected to sit alone, so it was a surprise when Stacy slid in beside her. "Are you going to the party? I think you should. You need to have some fun, and you need to prove to everyone that you don't care what they think."

Vaughn sighed. "I don't know, Stacy. I think maybe I just want to go home and veg." Though she would never admit it, there *was* a pint of Ben and Jerry's ice cream in her freezer, and it was loudly calling her name.

"C'mon, Vaughn. Just stop by for a while. I'll give you a ride home if you want to leave early."

"All right," Vaughn agreed, though she had no idea why. She wasn't a drinker, and the party circuit had never been her scene. The party was being held in Neil Zucher's basement, and Vaughn breathed a sigh of relief. Neil's parties were generally tame. She grabbed a diet soda as soon as she arrived and stood at the periphery of the room, watching. She had learned a lot by watching her fellow classmates, and she hadn't been exaggerating when she told Danica she knew her secrets. She knew *everyone's* secrets.

A flutter of activity alerted her to the fact that Grant had arrived. She tried to melt into the wallpaper, but he spotted her as if he had been searching for her. The sight of him stalking toward her with his hand once again outstretched was enough to make her want to toss her drink in his face and run away. Instead she held her hands tightly curled toward her chest so he couldn't grab one.

"What is it now, Grant? Can't you just go away and leave me alone?"

"I just want to dance with you, Vaughn. Geez, lighten up."

"As if she could," an unknown football player muttered, snickering.

Smiling vaguely, Grant clasped her hand and led her behind him, weaving their way through the mesh of bodies that were pressed tightly together, either dancing or making out or both. At last he found a clear spot and faced her, resting his arms on her waist. Vaughn held her breath, waiting for his apology, but none came.

"Can you believe we're seniors?" he asked instead. "I can't believe it. Where did the time go? It's sort of sad, you know? People you've known all your life suddenly disappear into the ether."

"The ether being college?" she asked.

"Exactly," he said.

"Why do you suddenly care so much? I've never thought you were into school until this year."

"I probably wasn't. But with all my brothers at college, school has taken on more of a priority. I've actually been really lonely," he said, putting forth his bottom lip in the semblance of a pout.

"What about Ivy?" she asked. Ivy was his sister. A junior, she was a year younger, and she was beautiful, the sort of blond and perfect beauty that Vaughn longed for. Not that it did Ivy much good.

Vaughn regretted mentioning her name when Grant looked around the room, scouting for his sister. He found her standing in a corner, talking with Neil. "Neil," Grant yelled and shook his head disapprovingly.

Neil startled like a dog that had been caught with his head in the treat jar and quickly scurried away. Ivy sighed resignedly and leaned against the wall, staring at her brother with sad, resentful eyes.

"Poor Ivy," Vaughn said.

"What's wrong with Ivy?" Grant asked, puzzled.

"You wouldn't understand if I told you. Let's just say we're all pulling for her."

"Okay," Grant drawled. "Whatever." They swayed in silence for a while. It was nice to dance with someone taller, Vaughn thought. Who was she kidding? It was nice to dance with *anyone*. She hadn't danced with a guy since eight grade square dancing lessons in gym class. And when Grant was absent, she'd had to dance with someone a head shorter than her.

"You remind me of my favorite horse," Grant said thoughtfully after a long silence.

"What?" Vaughn asked, stopping short so that they bumped shoulders.

"Your hair—it's the same color as my horse's mane."

"Are you making fun of me?" she asked.

"No," he said. "I was just saying your hair is pretty."

"So comparing me to a horse is a good thing?" she asked, still uncertain.

"Of course," he said, as if the answer should have been obvious. "Do you use horse shampoo?"

Now she was sure he was making fun of her. "Grant…" she said, trying to pull away.

"Lots of girls do now to make their hair grow. I just wondered if you did. Ivy doesn't, but she probably would if Dad would let her. He buys this expensive shampoo, and he…" He trailed off, darting a glance toward the next room. "Want to go in there?"

Vaughn froze, turning to follow the line of his gaze. "There?" she asked, pointing toward the notorious and darkened makeout section of the party. "Do you know what's in there?" Had he mistaken the makeout room for the kitchen or something?

"It's not like you and I don't know each other, Vaughn. We met in kindergarten, you know, and we've basically had all our classes together since then."

Vaughn stared at him. Was Grant Honeywell asking her to make out with him? And was he doing it as poorly as it sounded? "Why?" she blurted.

"Why not? We're seniors and the year is almost at an end. Don't you want to look back and say you made out at a party with someone?"

"Yes?" she said, making it sound like a question.

He smiled looking relieved. "Okay, then. You go in while I distract Ivy, and then I'll meet you in there."

She paused, looking at him over her shoulder. "Why do you need to distract Ivy?"

"Because I don't want her getting any ideas about trying this sort of thing for herself," Grant said, sounding uncharacteristically stern. Vaughn laughed, and he smiled.

She turned toward the room, the butterflies in her stomach growing as she entered the room and stumbled toward where she hoped the couch was. The room was pitch black and the sounds some people were emitting were enough to tell her she didn't belong. *I'm only going to kiss him,* she promised herself, though she wasn't worried about Grant taking things too far. He didn't have that sort of reputation and neither had his brothers; their family was famously conservative in their values.

"Vaughn," Grant whispered.

"Over here," she hissed, her cheeks heating with a blush. She couldn't believe she was doing this. Why was she doing this? Grant was nice looking, but so were a lot of guys. Was it because he was the only one who asked? Was she that desperate?

"I brought you something," he whispered. "Hold out your hands."

Nervously, she extended her hands and felt something soft and furry. *This is weird,* she thought. She started to refuse the gift, but it was shoved roughly in her hands. She held it, trying to examine what it might be by feel.

The lights in the room were suddenly flipped on. Vaughn squinted against the darkness, blinded at first, but she could still hear, and what she heard was laughter. Again.

Opening her eyes, she saw that the thing in her hands was a stuffed horse, and it was wearing a girdle. Her girdle. She didn't stay long enough to see Grant's face after that. She simply tossed the horse away and ran from the house. She didn't stop running until she reached her home, three miles away.

CHAPTER 1

Grant caught sight of the woman and stared, not only because she was beautiful, but also because she was wearing red. A red dress, to be exact. He had always been partial to red, and he studied the woman, trying to figure out why she looked familiar when he was sure he had never seen her before.

One of her long and perfectly sculpted legs was crossed over the other, bouncing gently as if she were either nervous or impatient. She sat on a high stool at a tall table, slowly flipping the pages of a magazine. A mug of coffee sat before her, untouched. Though Lexington was not too far away and quite large, the lady was in Silver Springs, a suburb not many people went to unless it was on purpose.

Grant tried to remember the last time he had been so intrigued by the sight of a woman, but came up blank, which was a good description for his mental state. He wanted to talk to her, to say something clever, but the movie in his mind was a blank screen. At last he decided to go with the first thought he'd had about her.

"Are you lost?" he asked, peering over her shoulder to try and see what she was reading.

She looked up at him then and his breath caught. Her eyebrows were perfectly arched over chocolate brown eyes that were framed by long, thick lashes. There was something so familiar about her, but what? He couldn't place her, and it was driving him crazy. The feeling grew worse when she smiled, a secretive, amused smile that told him she knew more than he did.

"I'm not lost," she replied after allowing her assessing gaze to sweep him up and down. "Are you? I was under the impression your table was over there." She pointed behind him.

He frowned, perplexed. She had the accent of a local, and there was something familiar about her voice, but he still couldn't place her. "Yes, well," he said, flustered by his own confusion.

She smiled again. "I'm teasing you Mr., ah…"

"Honeywell," he volunteered.

"Honeywell," she turned the name over on her tongue with a thoughtful frown. "Aren't there a few other Honeywells around?"

"Just me and my brothers. We own a farm nearby."

Her assessing gaze swept over him again. "You're dressed awful fancy for a farmer," she said, affecting her drawl to remove the cultured edge.

"I'm going somewhere tonight."

"A date?" she guessed. She used her toe to push out the opposing chair, issuing an unspoken invitation for him to sit down.

He sat, shrugging out of his trench coat. He had only intended to stop in for a quick cup of coffee, not wanting to be late, but sitting here and talking with this woman seemed like a better option than what he had planned.

"It's my ten year high school reunion tonight."

"That's sort of a big deal. Are you nervous?"

"Nervous? Why would I be nervous?"

"Why, indeed?" she said. Her smile turned acidic for a second, but the expression was gone so quickly he was sure he'd imagined it.

"What are you doing here?" he asked.

"Having a cup of coffee," she said, glancing at her still-untouched mug.

"You came all the way to Silver Springs for the coffee?"

"It's the best coffee shop in town," she said.

"It's the only coffee shop in town," he replied. "Are you from Lexington?"

"Thereabouts, though I've lived in New York the last few years."

"Do you live there still?" he asked.

She shook her head. "I'm moving to L.A. I stopped in to visit my folks for a few weeks before I go. What about you? Have you always lived here?'

"I went away to college for four years, but then I returned."

"And what do you do?"

"I'm an engineer, though mainly I work with horses," he said.

"Why does an engineer work with horses?" she asked.

"Because my family's business is horses, but I've always been interested in all things mechanical. My degree has come in handy in a surprising number of ways, actually. Engineers make everything run smoother." He smiled at her, winking.

She smiled again, the smile that told him she was probably laughing at him, and Grant felt another flicker of confusion. "Did they teach you that line in college, Mr. Honeywell? Because I have to tell you that, in the real world, engineers aren't thought of as particularly smooth."

"What do you do?" Grant asked, bypassing her reply because he wasn't sure if she was making fun of him. It seemed like she was, but why would a total stranger be making fun of him?

"I'm a writer," she said.

"What type of writer?" he asked.

"For a few years, I wrote for a magazine in New York. Recently I've been writing fiction."

"Have you written anything I might have heard of?"

"Not yet," she said, and the acidic smile was back in place before quickly fading away. "But I have a feeling you'll be well acquainted with my work shortly."

Grant was a little dazed from watching her lips while she talked. She was so very pretty, and there was something magnetic and familiar about her, but what? It was driving him crazy. "Are you married?" he blurted.

She laughed and leaned forward, resting her elbow on the table and cupping her chin. "Is that some of that legendary engineering smoothness you were referring to? Because I have to tell you, Mr. Honeywell, that there are better ways to find out if a woman is attached."

"Like what?" Grant asked. "Teach me how a refined New York woman acquires such information."

"First you check for a ring." She leaned forward and glanced at his ring finger, smoothing over it with her index finger. "Then you check for a tan line. That tells you if the guy took it off to try and pretend he's not married." He noticed that *her* left hand was safely tucked under the table. "The other signs are more subtle. How often does his phone ring? Does he give you his number or insist on taking yours? Are his eyes darting around the room, checking out all the other women to see if there's someone more worthy of his precious freedom?"

"That sounds complicated. It seems much easier to simply ask," Grant said.

"You're just a simple country boy, huh?" she asked, resting her head in her hand again.

"Yes, ma'am," he said, mimicking her pose and leaning forward so they were only inches apart over the small table.

"Next you'll tell me that you've never broken any woman's heart," she said.

"Never," Grant said earnestly.

She stared at him for a few beats, smiling. "Wrong," she said at last, and then she hopped down from her stool and walked out of the shop.

CHAPTER 2

Grant sat staring at the door for a moment, almost like he expected the mystery woman to return. Why hadn't he gotten her name or asked her where her parents lived? He should have asked her out. He should have done anything other than sit still like an idiot and watch her walk away.

With a resigned sigh, he stood and put on his trench coat. He hoped he wouldn't be the only one at the reunion wearing a suit. It was being held at the town's only fancy restaurant, the only one with a ballroom. It was the same place prom had been held ten years ago. Grant wasn't one given to deep thoughts, but he felt a pang of nostalgia as he thought of his classmates. He hadn't kept in contact with anyone. Some kids, like him, had never left. He was friendly when he saw them, but he hadn't been particularly attached, preferring instead to hang out with his brothers. Who needed school mates when he had four built-in best friends?

His senior year he had come close to making friends, and the memories from that year were the one he treasured. His four older brothers had all been away at college, leaving him and Ivy alone. Suddenly his friends and his basketball teammates took on a whole new meaning, and he began to understand why people were so vested in their school friends; it was because they had no one else.

He would go to his reunion tonight, and he would enjoy it, and then he wouldn't think about it again. It wasn't his way to dwell on things or feel them deeply. He prided himself on being a "live in the moment" type of guy. He was twenty eight and had no regrets. Of course he also had no future, but he wasn't worried about that, either. Something would work itself out; it always did.

The banquet hall was already crowded when he arrived. He said hello to a few people whose names he couldn't remember, which was made more awkward by the fact that they introduced him to their spouses. He had never been good with names. At least he didn't have a spouse or date and therefore had no need to try and make an introduction to someone he didn't remember.

He circled around the room, talking to people. He stopped at the bar to grab a soda. Someone smacked him on the back and teased him about being a teetotaler.

"I thought college would have cured you of that," the guy, whatever his name was, said.

"College proved to me there's a good reason I don't drink. Four years in a frat house should be enough to make anyone commit to being stone cold sober," Grant said. "And until they invent an alcohol that doesn't turn the drinker into an idiot, then I guess I'm stuck with soda." He tipped his cup toward the speaker and took a sip.

The guy gave him a congenial smile and turned to face the opposite direction. "Whoa," he said.

His tone was universal male code for "Look at that woman," so Grant turned, too. And there she was, his mysterious woman in red. But what was she doing here? "Who is she?"

"I have no idea, but I want to meet her," the guy said. Grant watched as he took off his wedding ring and tucked it in his pocket.

"No good," Grant said. "She'll check for a tan line."

The guy grimaced and took out his phone, presumably checking to see if his wife had called. Grant stood back, resting his hip against the bar. This was going to be good. "Good luck," he said, nudging the guy toward the woman.

He watched as the guy approached and said something that made the woman laugh. *Smooth,* Grant thought. *Obviously not an engineer.* Then he took out his phone and checked it again, and the woman narrowed her eyes, glancing at his ring finger. Grant chuckled and the woman turned, zeroing in on him. He tipped his cup of soda to her and winked. She rolled her eyes and smiled. Turning, she said something dismissive to the guy and then walked away, not just away from the guy, but away from Grant, too.

Grant frowned. He had been hoping the woman would come talk to him, but obviously that wasn't her plan. Now he had to think of something to say to her, and he wasn't good at that sort of thing. It was uncanny how right she was; he wasn't smooth at all. He never had been. He wasn't the guy who said lines that made women laugh. He was the guy who blurted whatever he was thinking or feeling, usually offending someone so they wanted nothing more to do with him.

He remained at the bar and watched as the woman circulated around the room. Wherever she went, people's faces lit with surprise before fading to recognition. Okay, so she had obviously gone to school here, but Grant still couldn't place her, and it was making him crazy. The guy who had tried to gain a foothold with her returned and ordered a drink.

"No luck, huh?" Grant said, his tone sympathetic.

"No," the guy said. He sounded miffed as he put his wedding ring back on. "I should have gone for her in high school, but who knew she would turn out to look like that?"

"Who is she?" Grant said, unable to hide his desperation to find out the woman's name.

The guy looked up at him in amusement, probably enjoying his misery. "That's Vaughn Drake. But good luck gaining a foothold, buddy. Apparently she's a stone cold ice princess now." He threw back his beer and took a long drink as Grant turned to stare at Vaughn.

"That's Vaughn?" he repeated.

The guy pulled his beer from his lips and chuckled. "Oh, yeah, that's Vaughn. Who knew, right?"

Grant didn't reply, he simply kept staring at Vaughn. He thought maybe she knew it, too, because every once in a while she turned slightly in his direction, enough to catch him in her peripheral vision. And then she smiled, knowingly, triumphantly.

He wished now more than ever that he had some smooth line to say, something suave that would knock her socks off and impress her. He took a couple of steps away from the guy until he was out of earshot, and then he pulled out his phone and called his brother.

"Darcy, I need a line."

"You're going to have to clue me in here a little bit, Grant," Darcy said. "Like fishing line?"

"No, like a line to pick up a beautiful woman. Something good, not something cheesy."

"I never used a cheesy line in my life," Darcy said, sounding mildly offended. Another voice murmured in the background. Grant guessed it was probably Darcy's wife, Genevieve, disagreeing with him. "Did not," Darcy said, confirming Grant's guess. "Anyway, tell me a little more about the situation. Who is the woman? Where did you meet her?"

"High school."

There was a pause. "You know if you ask out a high schooler, the family will be run out of Silver Springs with pitchforks."

"No, I mean I knew her from high school. She's my age. It's Vaughn Drake."

Darcy's "Oh," was significant. "None of us has ever married anyone our own age before. That'll be a switch."

"I can't marry her if I don't go talk to her," Grant said.

"There. There's your line. Use that."

"You want me to talk about marriage?"

"Sure. You're going to marry her, aren't you? I mean, it's *Vaughn*."

Grant glanced at Vaughn and then got caught up staring at her. "If she's anything like she was ten years ago, then probably."

"Okay then. Go and claim your woman. Ouch. My wife would like me to point out that that was a misogynistic thing to say in front of our daughter."

Grant smiled. He loved his feisty, pint-sized sister-in-law. "Tell Gen I said she hits like a girl."

"Fat chance. Tell her yourself next time you see her, and then run like the wind."

Grant laughed and closed his phone, taking a deep breath before turning to approach Vaughn. He could do this. He took another deep breath when he reached her, and—hallelujah—she was alone. "So I was trying to figure out how I was going to marry you if you didn't tell me your name. And then, lo and behold, it turns out I've known you since I was five."

Vaughn looked up at him with a smile. "Now *that* was smooth. In fact, I think you just got yourself inducted into the engineer's hall of fame with that one. How are you doing, Grant?"

"Better now that I know who you are. Why the cloak and dagger routine in the coffee shop, Vaughn?"

She shrugged. "Turnabout and all that."

"You know I have no idea what that means," he said.

"Sure you don't," she replied.

He caught sight of the guy from the bar and nodded his head in his direction. "What's that guy's name?"

"That's Stuart," she said.

"Stuart," Grant repeated. "He played football, right?"

"Yes, and he's as much of a jerk now as he was then. Consistency is important, don't you think?"

"I do think that. And Stuart over there is going to be very impressed if I somehow convince you to sit with me and eat supper."

"This is what your life has become—impressing a high school has-been?"

He nodded. "Definitely. In fact, when I woke up this morning, my one goal was to impress Stuart What's-his-name."

"Wow, that's some dream, Grant. Who am I to dash your hopes?"
She smiled.
He smiled.

His palm skimmed her back as he led her to a table, and the feeling was electric. Was this what people meant about love at first sight? Not that it was technically his first sighting of Vaughn, but it was his first sighting in ten years. This chemical reaction to her, though, that was something. Was she feeling it, too? If the way she was smiling and leaning into his touch was any indication, then the answer was yes.

A waiter came around and began delivering food. Grant noted with disappointment that the portions were small. Vaughn, though, only picked at her food.

"Aren't you hungry?" he asked.

She shook her head. "I think I'll stick with the salad. You want this?" She poked at her chicken, covered in some sort of sauce.

"You should eat it," Grant said. "It's barely enough to keep a bird alive."

"I'm really not hungry, and you could probably eat four times this much."

"More like five," Grant said, shoving his plate closer to hers so she could shovel her chicken and mashed potatoes over.

"Aren't you afraid that someday it's going to catch up with you?" Vaughn asked.

He shook his head. "I work too hard to ever get fat. People think we hire people to do the manual labor around our place, but they're wrong. We do most of it ourselves. It takes a lot of calories to keep me going." He ate for a while before realizing that doing so left no room for conversation. "So, New York. I don't know why I didn't think to look for you there."

"I'm sure you spent a lot of time looking for me," Vaughn replied dryly.

"I Googled you a few times," he said. "Nothing came up. What was New York like?"

"The total opposite of Silver Springs, Kentucky."

"You say that like it's a good thing."

"It's an excellent thing."

"What's wrong with Silver Springs? It's home," Grant said.

"I don't think you would understand if I tried to explain it. Suffice it to say I haven't suffered much homesickness."

That news wasn't music to his ears, but he stuffed down his disappointment by asking another question. "And now you're going to L.A. Are you nervous about that?"

"No," she replied. "I'm used to being on my own now."

"So there isn't anyone special in your life."

She gave him an enigmatic smile. "I have friends."

What did that mean? Male friends? Boyfriends? How was he supposed to find out if she was seeing anyone when she was being so secretive? But then look at her. Of course she was seeing someone. She was Vaughn, and she was amazing.

Their class president, whatever his name was, stood to welcome everyone and give out superlative awards.

"People actually do this sort of stuff?" Vaughn whispered. "I thought that was only in corny television shows."

Then the guy called her name, and all eyes were on her. "Most changed since high school—Vaughn Drake."

Vaughn's smile was brittle as she headed to the stage to receive her award, a gift certificate for Peggy's Diner, right down the street.

Grant won for least changed. He went up onto the stage and received his gift certificate, but his smile was genuine. He liked Peggy's. He and his brothers were finally allowed in there again after a long banishment.

Thankfully the awkward awards portion of the evening was over, and then a DJ began to play some music.

"What are my chances of getting you onto that dance floor?" Grant asked.

"Who are you trying to impress now?" Vaughn asked.

"Myself. I'm pretty sure you're way out of my league. This would really give me a boost."

"Still struggling with low self-esteem, Grant?" Vaughn teased.

"You know it. Every day's a battle just to get out of bed." His grin assured her that he was as self-confident as ever.

Vaughn turned to look at the dance floor. "No one else is out there."

"Have you ever known me to follow the crowd?" he asked. He stood, took her hand, and led her behind him to the very center of the empty dance floor. It was a moderately fast song, but Grant swayed her as if it were a slow dance.

"This reminds me of prom," he said.

"Your memory must be impaired. We didn't dance at prom."

"Why not? I looked for you, and I couldn't find you."

"That's probably because I wasn't there."

"Where were you?" he asked.

She glanced away. "It was so long ago. Who knows? Who did you go with?"

"No one. I met up with a group of friends from the basketball team and then ended up being their designated driver for after prom. It wasn't that fun, actually. I would have had a whole lot more fun if you'd showed up. I always had fun with you."

Her answering smile looked as brittle as the one she'd used when she won the certificate to Peggy's Diner. "Do you keep up with anyone from here?" he asked.

"Just my parents," she said. "What about you?"

"Not really. I'm still close to my brothers."

"The famous Honeywells," she said. "How are they?"

"Married with children," he said. "I'm the last of a dying breed."

"Your brothers actually got married?" she asked. "What about Ivy?"

"She was the first to go."

"I can't believe she pulled it off. How did she manage that?"

"She ran off with a Yankee," Grant said, still chagrined at Ivy's betrayal, even all these years later.

Vaughn chuckled. "Good for her."

"Why does everyone say that when we talk about Ivy?" he asked.

"No reason," she said. "What about everyone else? Did they marry anyone local?"

"Brent married Haley Griffin."

"I don't know her."

"That's because she's lots younger than us. She's only twenty two."

Vaughn's eyes bugged. "Whoa."

"Yeah, don't mention the age thing. It's still a touchy subject for him. Corliss married Allie Miller; she was our housekeeper's daughter."

"I vaguely remember Allie."

"Darcy married someone you don't know. He and Genevieve live in the mountains. Everett married Larissa Porter."

She quirked one eyebrow. "A Honeywell and a Porter?"

"She's not like the rest of them. You'll like her."

"You're talking like I'm going to meet them."

"You are, aren't you? How long are you going to be in town?"

"A few more days."

"That's plenty of time," he replied.

"For me to meet your family?" she asked.

He shook his head. "For me to convince you to stay longer." He tightened his arms and lost himself for a few beats, just looking into her eyes. Vaughn had always had killer eyes. He couldn't believe he hadn't recognized her immediately. "It's nice not to have to bend in half to look down at a woman," he commented.

"It's nice to be able to look up at a man," Vaughn agreed. "There aren't too many men who value height as an asset in a woman."

"It's never been a requirement before, but I'm thinking of changing that. This feels good. Maybe it's not just the height, though. Maybe it's you, Vaughn." He worried then that he was coming on too strong. His habit of blurting out exactly what he was thinking or feeling had driven more than one woman away. Vaughn, however, just smiled and nestled further into his embrace.

"I think we're becoming a very big source of speculation," Vaughn whispered.

"I couldn't care less," Grant whispered. They kept dancing, drawing further and further into their own little world until at last the ballroom had emptied out and they were almost alone. Grant walked her to her car, barely able to wait until he could get her back in his arms.

"When can I see you again?" His whisper was more fervent than he anticipated, practically smacking of desperation. But he was desperate to see her again, and he didn't much care if she knew it.

"I want you to do something for me first," she said. They were so close together that her lips were almost but not quite touching his when she talked.

"What?" Grant said as his desperation kicked up another notch. He had never wanted so badly to kiss someone before. What he really meant was, "Anything, I'll do anything, just please let me kiss you."

"I want you to read my book."

She was speaking with the lip whispers again, the kind that brushed his lips like angel wings, so it took him a few seconds to process her request.

"What?" he said, moving back slightly so he could see her.

"I want you to read my book," she said, louder this time. "It's important to me that you know who I am before this goes any further."

"You wrote a book?"

She nodded. "I have an extra copy right here." She took another step back, opened her car door, and pressed a book against his chest.

"Okay," he drawled. "I'll read your book. So when can I see you again?"

"How fast can you read?" she asked. Then, with a saucy little smile, she hopped in her car and drove away.

CHAPTER 3

The next morning Vaughn was in a dead sleep when she heard him.

"Vaughn? Where are you? I know you're in here."

She sat up, clutching the sheet in front of her chest. Her pajamas were modest, but not exactly something she would want Grant Honeywell to catch her in, which he was about to do any second because he was storming through her parents' house like a bull in a china shop.

At last he located her door and threw it open with a bang. He took two steps in before pausing, taken aback by the sight of her in her French poodle PJ's.

"What are you doing here?" she asked, immediately on the defensive because she knew exactly why he was there. Apparently he was a very fast reader, indeed.

He held up her book and shook it. "This is why I'm here. Is this your idea of a joke? What is this?"

"A New York Times bestseller," she said, crossing her arms over her chest and attempting to pin him down with an icy stare.

"People pay money for this drivel?" he said, looking at the book in his hands like it was poison.

"A lot of people. Enough to make it to the top ten for the past four months in a row. What's the problem, Grant?"

"You know what the problem is," he said. "The problem is that this entire book is about me and my family."

"The book is a work of fiction," she insisted.

"So these five Honeybear brothers who are so big and so dark they resemble grizzlies, that's coincidence?"

She nodded.

"And their little sister, Lily, the blond-haired, blue-eyed beauty who's as helpless as a mouse in a cage among her overbearing, brutish brothers, that's another coincidence?"

She nodded again.

"And the main character in this story, Violet, the hapless cheerleader who is constantly a favorite target of Grady Honeybear, that's not you?"

"Someone either has an inflated ego or a guilty conscience. I'm going to go out on a limb and say maybe it's a combination," Vaughn said.

"Get real, Vaughn. You wrote this horrible story about me and my family, and I want to know why. Why would you do this to me?"

She stood on the bed, dropping the sheet, and actually towered over him with the added height of the bed. "Why do you think, Grant?"

"I honestly have no idea."

"Don't play dumb. I know you're not."

"Believe me when I tell you I have been wracking my brain to try and figure out why you would do this, but I can't come up with a reason."

"Then you have a very short memory."

"What are you talking about?" he yelled. "Are you crazy?"

"No, I'm vindictive and a good writer. They say revenge is a dish best served cold, and I'm finding that to be true."

He blinked at her. "So, last night, that was just part of some game for you. You were playing me."

She nodded. "The same way you played me all those years ago."

"I never played you, Vaughn. I don't know what parallel universe you've been living in, but I was never there. Give my regards to my evil twin."

"That's great, Grant. Keep up the sweet yokel act. I'm sure someday you'll find some other guppy who will fall for it."

He looked at her in silence again, and she almost believed his innocent act. She steeled herself against him, however, remembering how shattered she had been all those years ago.

"I thought maybe you and I could have something special," he said at last. "And now all I feel is relief that I'll never have to see you again. You're one nasty piece of work, Vaughn Drake. I'm sorry I saw you again. Enjoy your revenge. I hope you choke on it." He tossed her book onto the bed and let himself out of her house.

Vaughn sagged to the bed, feeling oddly cold and empty. This was what she had wanted, though. The plan had gone perfectly. She had staked out his routine and knew he stopped at the coffee shop every day. So she had set herself up at a table and waited. There was a moment of panic when she wondered if maybe he would recognize her right away, despite her weight loss, but, no, Grant wasn't one who saw much past his own nose.

He had taken one look at her and been drawn in, exactly as she had hoped. That was the point where she had almost blown it, though, because it turned out that she was still as attracted to Grant as ever. How was someone so horrible also so beautiful? His award wasn't completely correct; he *had* changed since high school. Somehow, he had gotten even better looking. Maybe it was because he had filled out, looking less like a gangly puppy and more like a grown man. He was still hugely tall, but since he had added more meat on his bones, it wasn't as noticeable. And then there was that suit. Unlike most men who bought off the rack, she would guess Grant's suit had been handmade specifically for him because it fit him like a glove. He looked more like a business mogul than a horse farmer. Call her shallow, but she had a thing for men with good fashion sense.

She had wondered if he was now as suave as he looked but, no, he was still the same old Grant, bumbling through life with a charming innocence. The sweetness was a nice contrast to the devastating good looks, but Vaughn wasn't fooled. She knew it was all an act. Somewhere inside of Grant Honeywell beat the heart of a predator, and she was determined not to be taken by his charms again.

That had been easier said than done, though. Apparently she was as affected by his touch as much as his looks. For a little while when they were dancing, she had let herself forget the plan. She had forgotten everything except Grant. That had been nice. So nice, in fact, that she considered scrapping the plan altogether. When he walked her to her car, she considered giving in and letting him kiss her. They could have a fling for a few days before she headed to L.A, and then she would send him the book. Then she remembered her hurt and humiliation from all those years ago, the pain that was never very far from the surface, and she knew what she had to do.

He had read the book, but there was a lot Grant still didn't know. That's where phase two of the plan came into play, though now Vaughn found she didn't have much heart to go through with it. In fact, she was feeling a little bit of remorse. Not about Grant. No, he had that coming, and payback had been sweet. But she should have made the story about him and left his family alone. They were innocent in all this. Besides being fabulously wealthy and annoyingly good looking, they hadn't done anything to her. She would have to make some changes. But, hey, it was her book. How hard could that be?

CHAPTER 4

Something was seriously wrong with him. Grant lay there and thought of how he had told Vaughn that some days he could barely get out of bed. At the time he had been joking, of course, but now, four months later, it was actually true, and wasn't that pathetic? It was all because of *her*.

Before she came back, Grant had never had so much as a bad day. Happy-go-lucky had been the term most often used to describe him. Now he was mopey. He knew, and yet he couldn't seem to get over it, to get over her. And that was the worst part of everything. As much as he now hated her, he couldn't stop thinking about her. It was torture.

A glance at the clock showed him it was a half hour past his normal wakeup time. With a sigh, he slowly dragged himself out of bed and stood up. Everything hurt. Was he supposed to feel like this at twenty eight? Life stretched out before him in a depressing array of days like this. All around him, his brothers were almost deliriously in love and, for the first time in his life, Grant was jealous. Again all because of *her*. Everything in life was now completely her fault, fueling his hatred even more. That was new, too. He had never hated anyone before. Hatred was wrong. But in the case of Vaughn, he couldn't help it. So great was his loathing that he had hung up a picture of her on the back of his door and now routinely threw darts at it.

The darts had hit it so often that there were gaping holes where her eyes and mouth used to be, but that didn't make him feel any better. And it didn't make him forget what those eyes and lips had looked like. How could someone so beautiful be so horrible?

He slogged through his morning routine, arriving too late for family breakfast. Who cared, though, when everything tasted like sawdust? He choked down a bowl of cereal—not realizing until it was too late that it was Allie's cereal and it was *healthy*. Gag. He carried his bowl to the sink, not waiting to say hello to their housekeeper, Julie, before he turned and walked to the stable. He wanted nothing more than to lose himself in his work today, but that was the problem when one chose to work with horses. The hands were kept busy, but not the brain, allowing plenty of time to think. And these days thinking was torture.

What he needed was a challenging project. Maybe he would finally embrace his inner nerd and build a robot. That way he could keep his mind busy thinking about plans and give himself something to do with his evenings. But then when it was finished he would just be a sad man with a robot. There had to be something else on the farm he could mechanize. What was the point of having an engineer in the family if he couldn't make things more efficient? Tonight after work he would take inventory and see what needed to be done. Surely he could come up with something he could make better. And if not, well, then maybe it was time he went to visit Ivy. The Kings might need some work done. Raising cattle was a much more mechanical process than raising horses. Surely he could find something there to keep himself busy. Maybe the change of pace and scenery would do him some good.

When he walked into the office, three of his brothers and his nephew, Owen, were waiting for him. He knew they were waiting for him because they turned to look at him as a unit.

"Sit down, Grant. We need to talk." This came from Brent, the oldest, telling Grant that it was something serious. Brent was the one in charge and whenever he imparted information, it was usually monumental.

"What is it?" Grant said, sinking into a chair. "Is Ivy okay? Darcy and Gen? Genevieve's not sick again, is she?"

"No, it's nothing like that," Brent waved his hand dismissively. "It's about you. And Vaughn."

Grant's expression darkened to a scowl. "I don't want anyone in this house saying that name ever again."

"Okay, but some information has come to light, and you need to hear it," Brent said.

Grant, idiot that he was, felt another instant of panic. "Is she okay? Is she hurt? Did something happen to her?"

"Yes, but not how you think," Brent said. "She's okay, I guess. It's just…You know how Haley likes to read the celebrity magazines?"

Grant smiled. His little sister-in-law was a sucker for the celebrity rags, but she kept them hidden as if they were a shameful secret. "Yes," he said.

"Well, Vau—*she* was in one."

"She was?" Grant asked. His stomach clenched and pitched. "Is she dating a celebrity?"

"No, she is one," Brent said. He reached behind him and pulled out a magazine. "And there's more. Apparently she sold the movie rights to the book." He didn't have to clarify which book. "They've started filming the movie. The good news is that the Honeybears are all nice looking men."

Grant blinked up at him in shock. How could he find anything about this situation funny when their family was about to be dragged through the mud? And not just in print, but on film, too. "I can't believe you're laughing at this," Grant said.

Brent's smile faded. "I'm sorry for you, Grant. You know that. I would never find anything about what she did to you amusing. But the part about us is pretty funny." He chuckled again before wiping the smile off his face.

"She makes us look like a bunch of moronic thugs," Grant said.

Brent shrugged. "That's nothing more than people already think we are. And, until lately, we didn't do much to change that image. To a high school girl who didn't know us, I'm sure that's how we appeared."

"But she did know me," Grant said. "We were friends, or so I thought."

Brent sighed and sat down, leaning forward. "She seems to have a whole lot of resentment. What exactly happened between you two?"

"I have no idea," Grant said wearily, swiping his hand over his face as he sighed. "She was always so sweet. She was the one girl who could always make me laugh, and she is the dead last person I thought would turn out like this." He picked up the magazine and began thumbing through.

"I'm not sure you want to do that," Brent warned.

"Neither am I," Grant said, but he didn't stop looking. And then he saw it. Vaughn, breathtakingly beautiful as she smiled up at a man who could have been his doppelganger. He read the caption, not realizing as he did so that he was holding his breath.

"Vaughn Drake, author of the wildly popular *Honeybear Chronicles*, standing with Joe James who plays leading man Grady Honeybear. Romance rumors have been swirling, but Drake's publicist insists the two are 'just friends.'"

"No," Grant said. The magazine fluttered to the floor as he shot to his feet.

"No what?" Corliss asked.

"No, she is not going to carry on a fling with the movie star version of me. No she is not going to make a movie about our family. No. Just no."

"What are you going to do?" Everett asked.

Grant swallowed hard, looking around at his family. The only person whose outrage mirrored his was Owen, but, at seven, he tended to reflect what anyone else in the room was feeling. Even if everyone else wasn't upset, they should be. It was his acquaintance with Vaughn that brought this mess upon their heads, and he wouldn't allow her to drag his family name through the mud. For the first time in a very long time, he actually felt like crying.

"I'm going to go there, and I'm going to stop this," he said. He looked at Brent again, their family lawyer. "Can we sue? She as much as admitted to me that this book was about us."

"I'll look into it if that's what you want. But, Grant, be sure that's what you want. Lawsuits can get ugly and expensive. If we decide to do it, I'll have to pass it off to someone more experienced in trial work."

"Allie?" Grant said.

"Allie's a prosecutor," Brent pointed out.

"Good, because I want to nail her to the wall. I want to make her pay. First things first, I'm going to go and see her and leave her no doubt about what I'm going to do to her. She thinks I was mean in high school? She hasn't seen anything yet." There. The moodiness was gone. Apparently the cure was a hefty dose of rage.

CHAPTER 5

Home. Finally. No one had told Vaughn that making a movie could be so exhausting, but it was. She had been on set for sixteen hours, sixteen frustrating hours. Despite the fact that she wrote the book and the screenplay, she had far less input than she wanted on the movie. In fact, it felt sort of like a runaway freight train about to knock her down and drag her along for the ride. What was it John LeCarre had said? "Having your book turned into a movie is like seeing your oxen turned into bouillon cubes." How very apt.

Today's frustration had been about Grant again. No, *Grady*. She had called him Grant a few times by mistake, earning herself some strange looks from the other cast members. Actually, it wasn't Grady who had been the source of her ire, but rather the director, TJ.

"I think we need to play up the romance between Violet and Grady," he had said.

"What romance?" Vaughn had replied. "There is no romance. She hates him; he's horrible to her."

"Really? I don't get that at all. I think they like each other."

"Trust me—they don't," Vaughn had snapped.

"Intentional or not, there are undercurrents there. I think we should explore them a little more. Audiences love a good love story."

"But the love story is between Violet and Baxter," Vaughn had said. Baxter was her dream man, a purely fantasy creation from her head. He was loving and thoughtful. He never called her an Amazon or showed her underwear to the entire student body.

"Yeah, I guess. But, no offense, the Violet/Baxter romance is sort of weak. The Violet/Grady thing works much better. They have chemistry."

That was the exact moment when Vaughn had developed a migraine. Her headache had lasted all day and, miraculously, eased up when she arrived home. She lay on the couch, too tired to get up and go to bed. The house, located in the exclusive Brentwood neighborhood of LA, was very nice, but she still wasn't sure if she wanted to buy it. For now she had a six month lease, leaving her two months to decide.

The panache of living here was a lot of fun. Reese Witherspoon lived on the next street, for goodness sake. But was this where she wanted to spend the rest of her life? She had been so busy working on the movie that she hadn't had much of a chance to settle in or make friends. While New York had felt like a bunch of smaller neighborhoods all strung together, LA felt vast and spread out. And it was hot with a capital *H*. It was barely fall, and already Vaughn missed the changing seasons of the eastern United States, especially Kentucky.

She would never admit it to anyone, but going home had felt good. Kentucky really was beautiful with its rolling green hills and white-fenced horse farms. Thinking of horses made her think of Grant, but she quickly shoved him out of her mind. That bridge was burned now; it was best to let it go. In all likelihood she would never be able to go home again in case she ran into him. She would have to fly her parents to see her, wherever she ended up.

Heavy pounding on her door alerted her to the fact that she had drifted off. She sat up in alarm and checked her watch. It was one in the morning. Shakily, she reached for her phone, thinking the only person it could possibly be was her publicist with some type of emergency.

"Hello," Axle answered, sounding alert and chipper as always.

Vaughn wasn't sure if he actually didn't sleep, or if he just liked to give that illusion.

"It's Vaughn," she whispered.

"I know, darling, I have caller ID."

"Are you standing on my front porch?"

He laughed. "Do you want me to be?"

That was certainly an interesting question, but one she had no time for right now. "Will you stay on the phone with me for a minute while I see who it is?"

He must have picked up on the tremor in her voice because his amusement faded away and he was suddenly all business. "Maybe you shouldn't answer it, Vaughn. Call the police. Or maybe it's the paparazzi." Was it her imagination, or did he sound slightly enthusiastic over that thought?

"Why would the paparazzi be hounding me at one in the morning?" she asked as she crept cautiously to her door.

"I think they sleep during the day so they don't miss any nighttime action," Axle said. "I have my other phone in my hand. Let me know if I need to call the police for you."

"Okay," she said. Standing on her toes, she peered through the window at the top of the door. She would only be able to see whoever it was if he or she was tall enough to be seen over the top of the fan-shaped window, but that wasn't a problem. Vaughn didn't realize she was frozen in shock until Axle's voice snapped her to attention.

"Vaughn, darling, are you okay? Is it a homeless person or a burglar?"

"No, it's something much worse," Vaughn said. She sighed. "It's fine. It's someone I know. Thanks, Axle." She hung up, ignoring his continued questions, and then opened the door to a very angry Grant Honeywell. The best defense was a best offense; hadn't she heard that somewhere?

"What are you doing here?" she snapped. "How did you find this address? Did you hire a private detective? Are you having me watched?"

His scowl turned impressively darker. "Whoa, simmer down there,

Secret Squirrel. I went to your house and asked your mother where you live like normal people do."

She crossed her arms over her chest. "What are you doing here? What do you want?"

"You know why I'm here."

For one wild second, she thought he might tell her that he hadn't been able to stop thinking about her, that the evening of the reunion had meant so much to him that he had decided to overlook the book and pursue her instead. Then reality came crashing back.

"I'm here to deliver this cease and desist letter from my attorney. Stop filming your little movie, or I'm going to sue."

He shoved a letter into her slack fingers, and the bottom dropped out of her stomach. He didn't really mean that, did he? She hadn't pegged him as the litigious type, but maybe she had underestimated his anger over the book.

"The book is a work of fiction," she said.

"And I'm my Aunt Sally," Grant said.

She rolled her eyes at his charming vernacular. It had been a long time since she heard someone talk like the people she was used to back home. In fact, she was pretty sure she had all but lost her accent, and she never said "y'all" anymore.

"The book and movie are airtight. I made sure of that with my attorney."

"Sounds like you were intending to get sued," he said. "That proves my point and adds to my case."

"It's standard procedure," she lied. Since it was her first book and her first movie, she had no idea what standard procedure was. But she had learned early that covering her backside was vitally important in this business. Of course at the time she never thought she would have to cover it from one of Grant's advances. Maybe it was ridiculous, but she felt a little hurt that he was threatening to sue her. Sure, he had tortured her in high school, but he hadn't been vindictive. Suing her was definitely vindictive. Maybe if she talked to him they could come to a peaceable solution.

"It's late," she said. "Too late for you to find a hotel. Why don't you come in? You can stay in one of my guest rooms, and we can talk about this in the morning."

"I'm going to sleep in my car," he said.

She glanced behind him to see a tiny subcompact rental car. He probably had to form some acrobatic feat just to get in the thing, let alone sleep in it. "That car is too little. I have a king-sized guest bed."

"What does it tell you, Vaughn, that I would rather sleep in a pretzel formation in that little car than sleep in luxury accommodations under the same roof with you?" He scanned her up and down, his lip curled in disgust, and then he turned and walked to his car.

Ouch, Vaughn thought. She closed the door and was surprised to feel the sting of tears. Over the years Vaughn's hide had toughened considerably. In fact, most people thought her outer shell was impenetrable. She had been yelled at by the best in the business and never batted an eyelash. Why was it that a few soft-spoken words from Grant Honeywell were working their way behind her hard-earned defenses?

I'm tired, she thought, trying to remember the last time she'd had a full night's sleep. Tonight wouldn't be any better. She had to be on set at six, which meant she had to wake before five. The studio wasn't too far away, but L.A. traffic was a nightmare. Ten miles of driving could easily take an hour. The good part about being so exhausted was that she fell into bed and crashed, not giving the giant man in her driveway another thought until her alarm buzzed a few short hours later.

Then she stumbled groggily to the shower and hopped in, waking slightly under the hot spray. There would be time for breakfast later, and she could apply her makeup while sitting in traffic, so she blow dried her hair, got dressed, grabbed her coffee, and walked out the door. And that was when she remembered Grant. If she hoped to slip by him unnoticed, it was a vain hope. Either he hadn't slept or he had a sixth sense about when she would wake because when she walked outside of her house, he was leaning against his car. It was so small the top barely reached his shoulder.

"Was that all you could get?" she asked.

"No, I enjoy muscle cramps," he answered, sounding grumpy and only half awake. He surprised her by reaching out to take her coffee and drink some before handing it back to her.

"Well, I would say it was good to see you, but that would be a lie."

"I didn't think you had a problem with lying," he said, arms crossed over his chest and an impressively scary scowl on his face.

"Let's not do this. You came to say what you had to say. Goodbye. Safe journey back to Kentucky."

"No," he replied. When he reached out, she thought he was going for her coffee again, but instead he grabbed her, opening the back door of his tiny car and shoving her roughly inside. Of course she had no intention of staying there, but when she tried the handle, it didn't budge.

Grant went to the driver's side and eased his way in. "Ever since I became an uncle, setting the child safety locks has become second nature," he said, sounding markedly more cheerful now. "Where to?"

"Nowhere. You cannot come with me. It's a closed set."

"You're the writer. Aren't you allowed to have guests?"

"Yes, but not you," she said.

"Well, now, I guess you have a choice to make. We can sit here all day, or you can go to work. With me."

"You can't kidnap and manhandle people this way," she said, chagrined when her long-dormant accent suddenly flared to life.

"Sure I can. I'm a brutish beast of burden, at least according to you. Why not act like what you think I am?"

Vaughn took a deep breath, counted to five, and released it. "Grant, this is not Kentucky. This is LA. I can't just show up with someone from my past who looks exactly like the main character in this movie and not expect people to ask questions."

"I would be really happy to provide people with an answer to any questions they might have," Grant said.

I'll just bet you would, Vaughn thought, feeling a disaster in the making. What could she possibly say to get out of this awkward situation? "Look, I'll make a deal with you. I'll let you come with me to the set today on the condition: that you don't talk to anyone or say anything about who you really are."

Grant chuckled. "I'll make *you* a deal. I'll get you some lunch and let you have one potty break every four hours. It's bound to get cramped back there, and ladies have needs."

Vaughn squinched her eyes shut and ground her fists into the sockets. It was high school all over again. She had worked so hard to take control of her life. What was it about this man that made that control seem like a gossamer illusion? "You can't do this," she said, a whole lot of desperation in her tone.

"Watch me," Grant said, sitting back and closing his eyes. "I could use some more sleep anyway. Maybe you should get some rest, too. Those bags under your eyes need some attention."

That comment made her so angry that she looked around the back seat for a weapon, finding none. Tossing hot coffee in his face might be a nice touch, but with her luck he was impervious to pain and would only think up some further punishment for her. She blew out a breath, hating what she was about to say. "Fine. Take me to the studio."

"Yes'm," he replied, all humility now. He started the car and she gave him directions. There were large gaps in conversation while they sat in traffic. During those times, he reached his hand over the seat for her coffee. She wanted to tell him no, but she was already too exhausted to argue with him. It wasn't yet six in the morning, and he had beaten down her defenses. She was suddenly glad he was going to be there today. Let him see in person a reminder of his handiwork. Maybe it would open his eyes to how horrible he had been in high school.

While he drank her coffee and her hands were free, she pulled out her makeup bag and began to work on her face. Once she looked up to catch Grant watching her in the rearview mirror, but he quickly schooled his eyes forward again. She smiled smugly, secure in the knowledge that, despite his protests, he found her attractive. *Ten years too late, buddy,* she wanted to say. *You should have been nicer to me when I was fat.*

The car came to a sudden halt, causing the mascara wand in Vaughn's hand to swipe jaggedly across her cheek. She looked up, expecting to see another traffic jam, but there was nothing.

"Oops, sorry," Grant said, an unrepentant smile on his face.

She held back her retort and took out a makeup remover wipe, glad she kept them in her handbag. So maybe he wasn't exactly bowled over with attraction for her. He kept her coffee, drinking the rest of it, and Vaughn started to develop a caffeine withdrawal headache. At least there would be coffee on set. Thinking about work made her apprehensive about Grant's presence there today.

"Grant, you're going to need to stick close to me today," she told him.

"What's the worst that could happen if you let me out of your sight?" he asked.

"You could walk in on a live taping," she replied, trying to sound severe.

"Golly, ma'am, I never realized how much I needed a keeper before," he said, affecting his accent to a deep drawl. "How have I survived these twenty eight years without you?"

"I'm just saying that you're new to this." The truth was that she was nervous someone would see him or hear him talk or ask him his name and figure out the truth—that the story was true and Grant was the main character. She was finally, blessedly, in control of her life. She didn't want or need the humiliation of people finding out that the trauma of Violet's high school life was actually the true story of Vaughn's life. Awkward.

"I think I can handle walking and talking, thank you very much, Vaughn. Despite your opinion I am not a moron. And I'm not new to California. My degree is from Caltech."

Vaughn was impressed and surprised, but she tried not to let it show. Caltech in nearby Pasadena was one of the best engineering schools in the country. She had never pictured Grant attending college so far from home. Rather, she had pictured him still living with his parents and earning a degree from a nearby community college.

"Why didn't you stay here and use your degree?" she asked.

"Because I was needed at home," he said shortly.

"Did you like it here?"

He shrugged. "It was nice. But I tend to be happy wherever I am at the moment." He darted a narrow-eyed glance at her in the rearview mirror. "Usually."

Meaning he wasn't happy now with her. Ouch. "So, what, your parents just use you as a work horse, despite your own dreams and ambitions to the contrary?"

"No, Vaughn, my parents told me to do whatever I want with my life because they're that sort of people. But I am put aside my own dreams and ambitions to do what's right because that's the sort of man I am. We're here. You can stop talking now." He turned to glower at her over the seat. "And stop talking bad about my family. They've done nothing to you."

Vaughn resisted the urge to be intimidated. "Someone's touchy this morning. You know that sort of sensitivity usually indicates that I've hit a nerve. Maybe all isn't well in Honeywell land. What is it, Grant? Did your brothers pick on you when you were little? Are you jealous of their wives and children?" In truth, she had nothing against the Honeywells and she didn't really think anything bad was going on in their family. It just felt so good to be able to push Grant's buttons for once. He seemed so unaffected by everything. Apparently his family was the one thing guaranteed to get to him.

"Enough!" Grant roared. Leaning farther over the seat, he was very close to her face when he said the next part. "Don't talk about my family ever again." He enunciated each word as if it was followed by its own period. "Whatever petty grudge you have against me is fine, but I won't have them a part of this. If you want retribution, Vaughn, then keep going because I promise you I won't stop until I take back every cent you have earned from this book and then defame you in every magazine. You think I'm stupid and don't know what's going on, but you're wrong. I'm warning you now to stop before this gets really ugly."

She had never seen Grant so angry before, and she never wanted to see him this way again. It was terrifying. She didn't fear for her physical safety because he wasn't the type to hit a woman, no matter what. But she suddenly had no doubt that he would follow through with his threat and make things very ugly for her. She had thought she was safe because his family's influence didn't extend beyond their tiny town in Kentucky, but what if she was wrong? What if the Honeywells had friends in high places who could make life uncomfortable for her? She had learned long ago, though, never to let anyone see her sweat, so she replied with a cold smile that belied none of her inner fear.

"If you're done being a caveman, then I need to go. I'm late for work."

He slid out of the car, slamming the door behind him. For a panicky moment she wondered if he was going to leave her trapped in there. She would no doubt die because it was already hot outside. But, no, he opened her door and even held out a hand to help her out. She ignored it, though it caused her to make an ungraceful exit from the tiny car as she attempted to unfold her long legs from the cramped space. Grant stood by, unabashedly staring at her legs.

"Having fun watching the show?" she snapped.

He shrugged. "I wish just wishing the inside of you looked as good as the outside. Too bad the pretty package is a cover for pure ugly."

"And you're so deep you're magically able to see beyond the outer package," she said, her tone dripping sarcasm. But she was infuriated beyond reason. In high school, she had been as sweet and innocent as pie, but Grant hadn't taken the time to see beyond her outer shell then. Who was he to lecture her now?

"I'd like to think so," he said sincerely.

Vaughn rolled her eyes. "You are so full of it, Grant."

"What is your problem, Vaughn? Why are you so angry?"

"Maybe it was all those years spent as the requisite fat girl. Believe me when I tell you men don't see beyond the outer shell. Don't try to pretend otherwise because we both know it's a lie."

He darted her a surprised sideways glance. "When were you fat?"

She laughed and rolled her eyes. "Nice try, Honeywell, but the innocent country bumpkin act doesn't work on someone who's known you for twenty three years. I bet it went over great at Caltech, though. I bet you had women eating out of your hand." She stopped short, biting her lip when she realized she almost sounded jealous. She definitely didn't want to go there.

"Not really," he said, sounding lost in thought. "I was…" he paused, clearing his throat. "Shy." He finished as if it were a shameful secret.

Vaughn didn't have a reply for that. Was he being sincere? The last few years of her life had made her naturally suspicious and distrustful of men, so it was hard to tell. The thought of Grant Honeywell being shy, though, was enough to melt her frosty heart, at least a little bit. "I have trouble picturing you as shy," she said.

"So did I before it happened. But I had never left Silver Springs or my family. It was strange to be somewhere so unfamiliar. People had no idea what a Honeywell was. I was just a face in the crowd, and it was hard to figure out who I was on my own." He was frowning, remembering.

She didn't want to feel sad for him, imagining him as a lonely and scared college freshman, but she couldn't help it. Somehow the stubborn vision of Grant, alone, lonely, and afraid, invaded her vision and lingered. "Didn't you have any friends?"

He shrugged. "A couple. I talked to a few people in my classes, but the people I wanted to be friends with didn't seem to want to be friends with me. The fraternity guys sought me out, but it wasn't really my scene. I was more attracted to the smart kids, but they shied away from me, thinking I was a partying frat guy. I never found my niche in college. It was a relief to go back home."

Vaughn reached up a hand to touch him and then came to her senses and let her hand drop lifelessly to her side. What was she doing? Had she really been about to offer comfort to Grant Honeywell? No, no, no. This was probably some advanced technique he had honed to get under her defenses. He was probably as popular in college as he had been in high school, and he had likely dated every woman in the school. She couldn't allow herself to fall for his act again. She should say something snide here, something to convince him that she was unaffected by his story, but she couldn't do it. The best she could do was remain silent and keep her hands to herself, something that was proving harder to do than it should have been.

For good measure, she tucked them behind her back, one firmly clasping the other to keep them in check.

CHAPTER 6

They walked on set and it took Vaughn only about thirty
seconds to realize Grant was no longer beside her. He was
6'8". How did he disappear into thin air like that? She stopped short,
surveying the horizon in panic. There was no telling what trouble he
could get into let loose on a studio lot.

"Something wrong, Miss Drake?" one of the production assistants
asked her.

"There was a man with me. Did you see which way he went?"

The assistant tipped his head in concern. "A man? I didn't see any
man. What did he look like?"

Exactly like Grady Honeybear's character. Yeah, there was no easy
way to explain this mess. "Never mind. If anyone is looking for me,
please tell him where to find me."

"Yes, ma'am," the assistant said, unable to refrain from giving her a
strange look as she passed by. She sat in her chair at the side of the
stage, picking up that day's script and shooting schedule to go over
any changes awaiting her approval. Not that it mattered much what
she said or didn't say. Her contract had been written in such a way
that her approval was a polite formality. The director was the one in
charge of any changes. Next time, if she ever sold movie rights again,

she would get an agent who was better versed in the ins and outs of the business. It was torture for Vaughn to sit by and watch while other people changed her story.

She had no idea how long she sat reading and making notes, but suddenly there was a hand under her nose, and it was holding coffee. She jumped, turning to look at Grant who was now seated beside her. Not only was he holding two cups of coffee, but his hair was wet, he was clean shaved, and wearing different clothes.

"How did you…" she trailed off, not sure which question should take precedence. How did you materialize out of thin air without making a sound? Where did you take a shower? Where did you find coffee? How did you know to fix it exactly the way I like it? That one was easy to answer—it was because he had drank most of hers this morning. That thought made her realize how badly she needed coffee right now. Setting aside her other questions, she gratefully took the coffee and almost gulped it.

"Thanks," she said after a few satisfying sips.

"You're welcome," he said. "I figured you needed some after I drank yours this morning. Muffin?" He reached in his pocket and produced a large blueberry streusel muffin.

Vaughn frowned. "No, and you can't just take those. They're for the cast and crew."

"I didn't just take it. Someone stopped me and offered me food and coffee."

"Why would someone offer a stranger food and coffee?" Vaughn asked.

He shrugged. "Maybe she thought I looked hungry. Whatever the reason, she was very sweet, and I appreciated it. Maybe not everyone here is horrible." He eyed her, letting her know without any doubt that she was included in the horrible category.

"She probably thought you were one of the actors," Vaughn said. "She probably thought she was doing her job by trying to feed you. You should have told her otherwise."

"Do you want me to pay for the muffin? Because I'm pretty sure I could spare the buck fifty," he said.

"It's the principle," she said, not sure why she was so intent on sticking to her guns on this one. The food was a free for all, and most of it got wasted at the end of the day. Grant could probably eat a dozen muffins and no one would notice.

"Please, Vaughn, lecture me some more about principles while we watch the unscrupulous movie you're making about my family."

They frowned at each other in a silent standoff until one of the PA's announced the scene. Everything became quiet as the marker was snapped and filming began. Of course today would have to be a scene that was specifically between Violet and Grady, a flashback to high school. On the one hand Vaughn was glad Grant would see how much his little stunt in high school had hurt her. On the other, it was awkward to have him see just how hurt she had been.

He stared transfixed at the actors as the Grady character stuffed a nasty letter in Violet's locker. He had just shut it when Violet caught him red-handed. He jumped and turned to face her, blocking her locker with his tall frame as he made awkward small talk. At last he backed away. Violet opened her locker and the note fell out. She read it, her heartbreak growing as the terrible taunts began to sink in, and then she slid down the side of her locker, rested her forehead on her knees, and cried.

To his credit, Grant looked upset as he watched the scene unfold. What would he say when the scene was cut and he could talk again? It turned out the answer was nothing. The PA called the scene, and Grant stood and walked away. Vaughn thought maybe he was getting some air, but, no, instead he walked over to the director and spoke. Vaughn watched, horrified, as he and the director began a heated exchange. What was he saying? Was he telling the director about the pending lawsuit? The director didn't look angry, though. He looked thoughtful.

After a few nods of his head, he looked up and asked Grant a question. Grant nodded and pointed to Vaughn. They both turned to look at her before looking at each other. Should she go over there? She knew the answer was yes, but she was powerless to do so. Instead she remained rooted to the spot, watching the nightmare unfold.

Grant finally stood back while the director called to Joe James, the man who was playing Grady Honeybear. He jogged over and held out his hand to Grant who shook it with a smile. They the entire trio turned to look at Vaughn before huddling together in a conference. After a couple of minutes, they called to Lisa Sharp, the woman playing Violet. She joined the huddle as they talked in low tones, occasionally darting glances at Vaughn. It was those glances that made Vaughn want to get up and go over, but then it was too late. The group broke up and Grant was walking away, back toward her.

"What was that about? What did you tell them?" Vaughn asked.

"The truth," Grant said.

"But what did you say? What did they say? What happened?"

"Wait and see," Grant said, settling back into his chair with a secretive smile.

Vaughn faced forward nervously, resisting the urge to fidget.

The PA called the scene and snapped the marker, only there was no repeat of the previous scene like Vaughn expected. Instead an extra, one who was playing the part of another cheerleader, stepped into view and stuffed the letter into Violet's locker. Then Grady arrived, a red carnation in hand, and stepped forward. He hunched down, listening as he tried to pick the lock. Violet stepped into view and he hastily hid the carnation behind his back.

"What do you want, Grady?" Violet asked, her longsuffering tone telling him she believed he was up to no good.

"I just, um, I was, you know, saying hi and stuff."

"By hovering around my locker?"

He nodded. "So, hi." His voice cracked and he smiled.

Violet crossed her arms over her chest in a defensive pose that Vaughn had used often. "Hi. Now go away."

"Well, I was…you know, today is…"

"Today is Valentine's Day. I know. So maybe you can give me a break and not be your normal self. Go." She made a shooing motion with her hand.

He nodded, backing away, being careful not to show her the carnation.

"No way," Vaughn murmured as soon as the scene was cut and it was safe to talk. "There is no way I am letting you get away with that." She turned to Grant and glared.

"With what?"

"With making Violet look like the bad guy. With making Grady look like some romantic hero. I'm going to talk to TJ and tell him I don't approve of this scene."

"You don't approve of the truth?" Grant said. His soft voice worked wonders to stop her in her tracks.

She swung on him. "That's not the truth; I should know—I wrote that scene."

"This is the truth; I should know—I was there."

"What are you talking about?" Vaughn asked, sinking weakly into her chair again.

"Valentine's Day sophomore year. The student council was selling red carnations, and I bought one for you. I was too nervous to deliver it in person, so I was going to break into your locker and leave it anonymously. And then you caught me and I lost my nerve, so I just ran away."

"You had time to slip the note in," she said.

"C'mon, Vaughn, you really think I would buy you a carnation and attach some stupid and insulting note to it? What would be the point of that?"

He had here there, but what he was suggesting was impossible. She knew the horrible note was from him. She had caught him stuffing it in her locker. Hadn't she? That part of her memory was vague. He had been standing there, for sure, but had she noticed the paper in his hand? Were his hands clasped behind his back like in the scene with Grady? Had he actually been holding a carnation? Or was this some trick he was using to once again break down her defenses?

"Right, Grant. Nice try. Why would you buy me a carnation?"

He shifted his gaze forward, staring at the empty set. "Because we were friends."

"Did you buy all your friends a red carnation that day?" she asked, not believing a word of what he was telling her. It was simply too far fetched.

"No, but I didn't have many girl friends. Mostly just you."

"You were friends with everybody," she said. Everyone had loved him. He had been the king of their school.

"That's not true. There were only certain people I considered actual friends, and only one of them was female. I could talk to you about stuff."

"What stuff?" she asked, trying to remember any real conversation they'd ever shared.

"I don't know. It's not like *I* have some weird diary where I recorded every conversation we ever had. I just remember being able to be with you the way I could be with my family. Comfortable. Fun."

That part wasn't so surprising. He *had* treated her like a sister, always teasing her. In elementary and middle school it had taken the form of hiding her possessions and pulling her hair. That stuff she could handle. It wasn't until high school the teasing had turned cruel. Thinking of all the ways he had tormented her, and especially that last time at the party, worked to ease her doubts. She snorted a laugh.

"I can't believe you almost had me with that. I don't care what you say. I know you're lying, and I'm not going to have this scene in my story." Determinedly, she stood and made her way to TJ, but he was full of congratulations for the new story addition. Apparently Grant had made it sound like the change was her idea.

"I'm glad you decided to go with what we talked about yesterday, Vaughn. I think we really need to play up the romantic tension crackling between Grady and Violet. Good call."

Vaughn wanted to lie down and throw a tantrum, right there in front of the fake lockers. How was she supposed to undo what Grant had done? Tell TJ it hadn't been her idea after all, even though he loved it?

"Who did he say he is?" she asked, gesturing toward Grant.

"Your creative collaborator. It's weird, though, he sort of looks a lot like Joe James."

Joe James, the actor playing Grady Honeybear. "Yeah, it's uncanny,"

Vaughn said. Defeated, she turned to look at Grant who gave her a smile and a wave while TJ went on and on, telling her how much he liked the new guy. Vaughn tuned him out while her mind stuck on repeat. *It's high school all over again. Someone get me a candy bar.*

She didn't eat a candy bar, though. Long ago she had overcome her tendency to eat her feelings. Instead she returned to her seat next to Grant and shook out exactly eight almonds from the bag she kept in her purse. He watched in silence as she ate them one by one and then put the bag away.

"Whoa, you must be stuffed after a meal like that," he said, frowning in disapproval. "Where's your real food?"

"That was it," she said.

"That wasn't enough to keep a gerbil alive."

"That was my mid-morning snack. I'll have lunch soon." *In one hour and thirty five minutes,* she thought, resisting the urge to check her watch. Food wasn't her friend. Food didn't make life better. Nothing could taste as good as being thin felt, or so she told herself. Daily. After years of searching, she finally found a diet plan that took off her excess weight, and there was no going back. The downside to the plan was that it was a bit stringent and skimpy, something she could usually ignore. But today Grant was staring at her in disapproval.

"Are you anorexic?" he asked.

"Rude," she said, glaring up at him. "Of course not. I'm just careful. Do I look anorexic?" She held out her well-toned arms for inspection. While she was slender now, she wasn't skin and bones. There was plenty enough flesh to cover her. In fact, she still had a little extra weight to drop.

"Yes," he said, sounding sincere. "You're almost six feet tall, Vaughn. You need more for breakfast than eight almonds and a cup of coffee."

"Thanks, doctor. I'll take your recommendation into consideration. Oh, wait, no I won't." For good measure, she frowned at him again.

"You wouldn't be so grumpy if you ate more," he muttered, facing forward and crossing his arms over his chest.

Vaughn could feel her frustration mounting. "If I'm grumpy, it's because you're here disrupting my life. And while we're on the subject of you disrupting my life, keep your comments about my food and my body to yourself. It's none of your business what I eat or how I look." She should stop there, but she was unable to keep herself from adding, "Besides, you didn't seem to have a problem with how I looked the night of the reunion."

"You've always been pretty," he said, surprising her. "You're a little too skinny now, but I was willing to make an exception. Note the past tense there."

She wanted to scream in frustration, but she couldn't, not least of which because it was time to film the scene again. So she sat back and tried to tamp down her frustration, but that was impossible to do when she was watching Grant's version of reality play out in front of her.

A little while later, she was horrified to realize she was biting her thumb nail. She quickly pulled her hand from her mouth and sat on it. *No, no, no.* How many years had it taken her to stop biting her nails? Now they were long, pretty, and expensively manicured. There was no way she was going to revert back to old habits just because she was having a bad day.

Her head swerved anxiously for the food cart. Where was lunch? Vaughn was so hungry she felt like she could happily sick her head in a trough. But when her food finally came, she took a deep breath, making herself wait an extra thirty seconds before opening it. Then, when she finally did open it, she took small bites, chewing thoroughly the way her trainer had taught her.

"Where's the rest of your lunch?" Grant asked. He had mysteriously scored not just one boxed lunch but two. The mystery was cleared up a little when one of their food people, a pretty young girl, delivered the boxes with a blush and a giggle. Grant had smiled at her and thanked her, his southern accent sounding extra thick, and the girl had practically fainted in delight. Vaughn had rolled her eyes, disgusted but too hungry to comment.

"I thought I told you to stop talking about my food," she said.

"That was an honest question. That's not really all you're eating, is it?" he asked.

She looked down at her salad. "What's wrong with it? It's the perfect balance of vegetables and protein with a teaspoon of grape-seed oil for flavor."

Without invitation he reached over and took a bite, grimacing as he swallowed. "Your definition of flavor is obviously different than mine. What kind of lettuce is that?"

"Arugula," she said.

"Tastes like what we feed the horses. And aren't you allowed to have any salt on that square inch of chicken?"

"Salt is bad; salt makes you retain water."

"Salt is delicious. Salt makes food not a punishment, which is what that is." He pointed at her salad again, grimacing. "Why do you eat like that? And don't say it's because you like it because that's just not possible."

She couldn't disagree with him because she didn't actually enjoy her food anymore. However, "Food is not meant to be enjoyed. Food is simply fuel for your body. When you put in better fuel, you get better results."

He blinked at her, either not comprehending her statement or not believing it. "Well that's the biggest load of hooey this side of the Mississippi. Food is not meant to be enjoyed? Are you crazy? Have you had pie? Because I'm pretty sure it's pure enjoyment."

"Yes, I've had pie. And ice cream, and cookies, and chocolate, and..." She broke off, remembering as the old yearning began to creep over her. She shook her head. "But that stuff is poison. That's how I wound up in the mess I was in. Now I feel great. I have more energy, and I look like this." She motioned to herself with her fork before taking another tiny bite of salad.

"Too skinny?" he said, and then hastily retreated when she narrowed her eyes at him. He held up his hands in surrender. "I guess that's your business if you want to look like that. My point is that enjoying food is one of the best parts of life. It's a little bit of heaven on earth. Without that, well, what's the point of eating?"

His words began to confuse her, but she couldn't let them. She had worked too hard. "Our culture is obsessed with food, and that's why our obesity rate is skyrocketing, not to mention diabetes."

"I'm not talking about junk food. I'm talking about real food, the kind your mamma makes on Christmas, the kind you dream about all year long, the kind that can make you weep with one bite. What greater joy is there than biting into a perfectly cooked steak, or spooning up a heaping mouthful of creamy mashed potatoes?"

None, Vaughn thought as the old longing rose to the surface again. This time it was much harder to subdue. "It must be nice to be a man and be able to eat whatever you want, whenever you want," she said sincerely. "I can't do that and look the way I want to look."

"Why? You were always athletic, and you're tall. You can probably eat more than the average girl. With a little work, you could be back to what you were in high school." He held out a bite of his sandwich to her.

It was like being tempted by Satan as Vaughn watched the juice drip from his sandwich and roll down his fingers. "I'm trying to avoid what I was in high school, Grant," she said. Her tone was probably more acidic than necessary, but, oh, that food looked so good.

At long last, Grant pulled the food out of her reach. "Yeah, I guess so. I guess nothing is the same with you as it was back then."

Vaughn watched as he ripped off another monster bite of sandwich, wondering why his tone had sounded sad. "I've worked hard," she defended. "Do you know how hard it was to lose forty pounds? I can't go back to the way I was."

"Here's the thing, though, Vaughn," he said as soon as he had chewed and swallowed. His eyes remained on his sandwich, and he spoke softly. "I liked the way you were then. I thought you were the most beautiful girl in the world."

CHAPTER 7

*V*aughn didn't have much chance to react to that bombshell statement because the food girl returned, and this time she was carrying a triple layer chocolate cake. She held it out shyly to Grant, the same way one might make an offering to a god. And he reacted appropriately, beaming at her and bestowing a "Thank you, sugar," that made the girl swoon from the charm of it all.

Though she knew she shouldn't watch, Vaughn couldn't seem to take her eyes off the cake as Grant scooped a generous portion onto his fork. The cake was so moist it stuck to the fork, and the icing was so chocolaty it looked like fudge. Somehow, he managed to get the huge bite to sit on his fork, but then he paused, turning to offer it to her instead.

"Want some?" he asked.

Get thee behind me, Satan, Vaughn thought as she pressed her lips together and shook her head. Frantically, her gaze darted away, resting on an actress a dozen feet away. There—that was why Vaughn didn't eat cake. The woman was willowy and slender, and probably a size zero. All in all, she was Vaughn's ideal. Women like her weren't tempted by cake. Women like her ate their tiny salads without complaint because they knew it was the right thing to do.

Maybe they didn't even eat salads. Maybe that teaspoon of grapeseed oil was too much fat and flavor for them. Maybe they sucked cardboard as a calorie reward. Who cared as long as the results were like that?

"I'm going to take a walk," Vaughn said. Her trainer had warned her of the dangers on a movie set. Not only was there every food she could think of, but she was mostly sedentary as she sat and observed, waiting to offer input and make script changes.

"Want me to come with you?" Grant asked. When Vaughn looked at him, she noticed a smear of chocolate frosting on his lip. Would he taste like chocolate if she kissed him now?

"No," she blurted, retreating a step until she bonked a light boom. "Just stay there." She turned and jogged away, running from the double temptation of chocolate and Grant.

People shot her odd looks as she sprinted from the building, her heels clacking loudly on the concrete. She stepped outside and yanked off her shoes, immediately regretting the action when her feet touched the burning pavement. She backed into the shadows and leaned against the wall, breathing hard to try and get a breath. Outside, the sun was so bright it was hard to keep her eyes open, and so she didn't. She closed them, tilting her head against the concrete wall. She had expected the concrete to be cool, but it wasn't. Maybe after so many sunny days it was impossible to find a cool spot anywhere. She never thought she would get tired of sunshine, but she was. It hadn't rained in four months, and Vaughn was at the limit of her sunshine endurance. She craved a good storm with a steady downpour.

Of course, that type of weather situation here would be a disaster. The ground was so parched that anything more than a brief shower would set off mudslides and floods. But, still, that was what Vaughn wanted. That and chocolate cake. Rain, chocolate cake, and Grant Honeywell. Just those three things, and her life would be…what? Better? No. A disaster, more like it. If it rained, the town would flood. If she ate the cake, she would get fat. Again. If she had Grant she would…what? She couldn't seem to find any way her life would be worse with Grant in it, and that disturbed her. Of course he was all wrong for her. He was a horse breeder from Kentucky.

But then a small little voice she had learned to ignore piped up to remind her that Kentucky was home. Home, with its rolling green hills and acres of white fencerow, horses, bluegrass, and southern charm. Oh, how she missed home.

I thought you were the most beautiful girl in the world. Grant's words returned to add to her torment. Had he really thought that? She, the too-tall, too-curvy girl who had been everyone else's doormat, had Grant thought that girl was beautiful? How could he like that girl and not the capable woman she was now? She was successful. She was famous. She was *thin!* Didn't her accomplishments account for anything in his eyes? He couldn't seriously prefer her mousy high school self to the confident woman she was today.

Only she wasn't actually confident. Her bravado was a show, but no one needed to know that. To the outside world she had learned how to project a strong, tough exterior, and she liked the person the world thought she was. The only person she didn't like was the person she actually was because, hidden somewhere deep inside, she was still the same old Vaughn, the chubby high school cheerleader who ate brownies every time someone said something mean that made her cry. Only now instead of eating brownies she did an extra half hour on the treadmill or bought a new pair of outrageously expensive high heels. She had a lot of heels.

"I can do this," she said out loud. All she had to do was get through the next few hours with Grant. Tonight, after shooting was finished, they would hash things out as much as possible. She would bite her tongue and allow him to speak his mind about her book, and then he would go home. Her life would return to normal—normal meaning once again under her rigid control. No more temptation, either in the form of food or Grant.

Her little pep talk worked to ease her away from the wall and back inside the building. She left her shoes off as she jogged back to the set, trying hard to make it before the break was over and the set closed for filming.

As she approached, Grant looked up at her with an easy smile before remembering that he was supposed to be angry at her. He then erased his smile and scowled, but the scowl looked unnatural on his face. *He's sweet,* she thought, and the realization disturbed her because it didn't fit with the fiendish mastermind she remembered from her childhood. It didn't really add up that someone who was so naturally kind, someone who was willing to have a fistfight if he saw an animal being mistreated, would also be the same person who was purposely cruel to a woman. And especially not when he said he thought that woman was beautiful. Which Grant was the true Grant? The sweetheart who loved puppies and thought she was beautiful or the bully whose sole purpose was to make her life a nightmare?

Until she was certain, she couldn't let down her guard and trust him.

"Darling."

Vaughn had just sat down when her publicist, Axle, called her name. She looked up with a smile. *Him* she trusted. He leaned in and kissed her cheek.

"What are you doing here?" she asked. She didn't fool herself that he had come to see her. She didn't rank high enough on his list of clientele.

"I had some business to tend to with Joe, and I couldn't leave without saying hello to my favorite writer." He beamed at her before turning his speculative glance on Grant. "Are you Joe's brother?"

Grant didn't like that question at all, Vaughn could tell. She preempted him before he could answer. "This is Grant Honeywell." She didn't have to elaborate more than that; Axle was the only person who knew all her secrets.

He arched a perfectly manicured eyebrow at her. "Really? What's he doing here?"

"He's here to put a stop to the nonsense," Grant answered. "If you'd like, I can show you a copy of the lawsuit I'm intending to file."

Axle gave him what Vaughn thought of as his million dollar smile. It could soothe the angriest celebrity, making them feel, at least temporarily, like the center of Axle's universe. "I'm sure we don't need to take things to court, Grant. We can settle this like gentlemen."

Vaughn held her breath to see how Grant would respond, but she didn't get the chance to find out because Axle's phone rang. By his expression and the total attention he gave to the call, she sensed a client was in trouble. He winked at her, waved to Grant, and then walked off, speaking soothingly into his handset.

"That man a friend of yours?" Grant asked.

Vaughn realized then that she hadn't introduced Grant to Axle. "Yes, sorry, I didn't get a chance to make the introduction. He's my publicist and friend, probably my best friend right now. It's hard to find people you can count on out here." She broke off, realizing she sounded pathetic.

"Axle," Grant repeated, turning the name over on his tongue. "That name is as fake as his accent. Has he ever even been to England?"

She was surprised Grant had seen behind the façade. Axle had most people fooled into believing he was London born and bred. "Not many people know this," she said in a conspiratorial whisper, leaning in so no one could overhear. "But his name is Bernie Goldstein and he's from New Jersey. He made up a persona for himself because he thought it would be better for business." Vaughn secretly thought he simply picked the person he had always wanted to be and become him. Who wouldn't prefer being a slick Brit to being just plain Bernie from New Jersey?

"Is that what you did?" Grant asked.

"What?" Vaughn asked, shifting uncomfortably as his eyes bore into hers, trying to read her soul.

"Did you come out here and forget you're Vaughn from Kentucky? Did you fool yourself into believing you're a fancy big city girl who eats like a rabbit and never has any fun? Because you're not. And I, at least, liked you better the way you were before."

"Who doesn't wish they could be somebody different?" Vaughn said.

"I don't," Grant said. "I like being Grant Honeywell."

"You would," she said.

"What's that supposed to mean?"

"It means you've never had a bad day in your life. You've never been the subject of ridicule; you've never known what it is to have people laugh at you."

"Oh, I don't know. It was a pretty bad day when I read your book. Imagine, stupid me, thinking I had found…and then realizing what you actually are. And I'm pretty certain Grady Honeybear is an idiot who everyone laughs at, and since he's me, and since the book has been read by millions of people, then I've been laughed at by half the world. Thanks to you. But I still have no desire to change who I am. I like who I am, even if you don't, even if the rest of the world doesn't. As long as I can look at myself in the mirror and like the man who looks back, then I'm happy to remain exactly as I am, fool or not."

But I do like you, and you're not a fool. It was on the tip of Vaughn's tongue to say the reassuring words, but she couldn't. She couldn't give him a foothold. She faced forward, arms crossed over her chest, and tried to block out his words. How long had it been since she liked the woman in the mirror? Had she ever? Had there ever been a time she looked at herself and thought, *You're all right, Vaughn Drake.* The answer to that was a resounding "no." She had always looked at herself and seen her glaring flaws.

She was too tall, too fat, too quiet, too submissive. Then she gave herself a makeover, inside and out, and she still didn't like what she saw. Now she was too abrasive, too standoffish, too cynical. And still too tall and too fat. Even though she had lost a lot of weight, she still wasn't where she wanted to be. All of a sudden she felt weary. She was tired of never measuring up to her own standards, and she envied Grant his ability to just live his life. He would probably fall off his chair if she asked him for pointers on how to make peace with herself, though. Imagining that cheered her immensely, and then they were saved from further conversation when filming resumed.

CHAPTER 8

$\mathcal{V}$aughn was exhausted. It had been another sixteen hour day of filming, sixteen hours of sitting beside Grant and trying not to absorb his open hostility, sixteen hours of watching gut-wrenching scenes from her adolescence played out for all the world to see. What had she been thinking, writing that stupid book? Had she hoped it would be cathartic, a way to heal, to finally put the painful memories from her past behind her? Instead it was reminding her of all the cruelty she had suffered at the hands of others. Today people labeled it as bullying and condemned it, but ten years ago it had just been normal life. Some kids were targets, and Vaughn had been a walking bulls eye.

Now the day still wasn't over because Grant was hungry, and he was taking her to dinner, somewhere he had eaten in college.

"Pinks?" she said, incredulous as they pulled up to the restaurant. "You hung out in Hollywood while you were in college?"

"I went where the food was," Grant said. "Their hot dogs are the best."

"I can't eat here," Vaughn announced. "I haven't had a hot dog in eight years."

"You say that like it's a good thing." He parked, ignoring her protests, and then came around to open her door when she remained seated. "I'm sure you can find something here to eat. Maybe they'll let you suck on a lemon."

She was too tired to argue, and too tired to care if she ate or not. But when they finally snaked their way to the front of the long line, she perked up considerably. They had turkey burgers. She ordered one plain and without bread along with a large water.

"With lemon," she added, resisting the urge to stick out her tongue at Grant. He, of course, ordered four loaded hot dogs. Vaughn tried to pretend she was disgusted by the overabundance of greasy food, but it smelled and looked delicious.

"Want a bite?" Grant offered when they sat down. "I won't tell." He leaned forward, holding out the hot dog to her and lowering his voice to a conspiratorial whisper.

"Not for all the money in the world," she said, leaning forward and matching his tone. "Stop trying to tempt me with your unhealthy treats. My body is a temple." She smiled, and he smiled in return before removing the hot dog from her face.

"It used to be," he said. "As well as my favorite preoccupation."

"Stop it," she said, sure he was teasing her. "You're teasing me, and that's just mean."

"I'm not," he said, holding up his hand like a boy scout taking an oath. "Why do you think I showed up at cheerleading practice every day?"

"To show us you were better at backflips?" she guessed.

He shook his head. "It was to watch you." He took a bite of hot dog as if he hadn't just dropped another earth-shattering bombshell.

"What are you talking about?" she asked. She picked at her turkey burger, instinctively knowing it was too good to actually be healthy. It was so flavorful it was probably loaded with salt and calories. She wanted to devour it. Instead she paced herself and nibbled. "You did not find me attractive in high school."

"No, you didn't find you attractive in high school. I happen to believe women should look like women. You, uh, had nice curves."

Was it possible Grant Honeywell was blushing? And was it

possible he was actually telling the truth? "Grant, I was overweight," she reiterated, almost hating to point out the obvious to him.

"No you weren't," he said, his tone vehement. "You're tall and athletic. You were the perfect size. There's a difference in being healthy and being fat. You were never fat."

She blinked at him. "You like fatties," she said, so shocked she couldn't contain it.

"I do not," Grant said, looking around in embarrassment at several overweight people nearby. "Good grief, Vaughn. Show some sensitivity."

"Me? These are my people. I was once one of them. You're the one who is making fun."

"How am I making fun?" he asked.

"By saying you had a thing for me in high school when I know for a fact that it's not true."

"You mean like all those facts that are in your book?" he asked.

"Yes, all those. I was there. I know what happened."

"You know what you think happened, but the truth is that nothing in that book is what really happened," Grant said.

"That's not possible," Vaughn said. "I know what you did to me, what you said about me."

"And how do you know?" he pressed. "Did someone tell you things I said?"

She nodded. "And then there were the things you did to humiliate me."

"Humiliate you? What are you talking about?" He sat dumbfounded, looking for all the world like he truly had no idea what she was talking about. She almost mentioned the fateful party, but she couldn't bring herself to do it. Instead she began with something simpler.

"You always singled me out and made me a part of your schemes."

"Because you were the only one game enough to be a part of them. I could always count on you to be fun. Other girls were so hung up on themselves or worried about what everyone else thought. You never seemed to care about that stuff, although I guess you did." He frowned, staring down at a blob of chili that had fallen off his hot dog. "I guess maybe all those years I got so caught up in the illusion of you I saw you as the person I wanted you to be, and not as who you really were."

For some reason, Vaughn thought it was one of the most painful things anyone had ever said about her, though she wasn't sure why. She looked to the horizon, squinting at the setting sun to cover the sting of tears in her eyes. They finished their food in silence, and she belatedly realized that they hadn't worked to clear any of the issues between them. His lawsuit remained unsettled. She had been hoping to have everything cleared up by tonight so he would go away, but that hadn't happened. And though he could well afford a hotel, she knew he would probably spend another night in his car. Call her an old softie, but she couldn't let that happen again.

"Grant, I want you to stay in my house tonight, and I don't want to hear any objections. I'm from the same place you are. I may have forgotten a lot of things from my upbringing, but hospitality isn't one of them, and I can't stomach the thought of you sleeping in your car again. So bring your bag because you're sleeping in there." She pointed to her large rental house.

"Okay," he said.

She opened her mouth, intending to argue some more before registering his ready agreement.

"It turns out I like comfort a whole lot better than sticking to my principles," Grant explained. "I haven't been able to bend my neck all day. Sleeping in that car practically killed me."

She laughed, some of the first genuine laughter she'd had in a long time. He smiled and they remained in the car just looking at each other for a few beats. Grant was the first to tear his eyes away. He cleared his throat.

"I don't know about you, but I'm zonked. Do you mind if we just go to bed?"

"No problem," Vaughn replied. "I'm exhausted."

Still, neither of them made any move to exit the car. It was an oddly intimate moment, confined in the small space and about to go into her house together. For years, no one but her parents had stayed with her, and she felt suddenly nervous about the impression she was about to make.

"I didn't decorate the house," she blurted when he put his hand on the door. "It's a rental, and it came this way. It's very modern. Modern is nice, but it's not exactly my style."

"What is your style?" he asked, tipping his head to the side as he studied her.

"Comfortable. Overstuffed couches with lots of color and texture."

He smiled. "I like that, too. Write this down—we have something in common."

She smiled. "Let's go to sleep before we find something else to argue about."

Still smiling, they walked into her house together.

In the morning, it wasn't the buzzing of her alarm that woke Vaughn, but rather the buzzing of her phone.

"'Lo," she mumbled, never having mastered the art of instant alertness.

"Darling, turn on the television."

"Axle," she said, though she knew it was him. Who else said "darling" at five in the morning? Vaughn sat up, feeling around her nightstand for her remote control. At last she located it, knowing instinctively to turn to the entertainment channel because Axle wouldn't be calling her about a world crisis. It had to be either something about the movie or something about her.

The sound was on mute, but as soon as the picture came into focus, she saw herself and Grant sitting across from each other at Pink's. The photographer had captured the exact moment they leaned over the table to talk to each other. They were smiling, and it was an intimate scene as if they were old friends, or more. Vaughn gulped, knowing Grant wasn't going to like this. He wasn't one who would enjoy publicity on any level, and especially not on this scale and, oddly, she agreed with him. Despite the fact that she was a so-called celebrity now, she preferred to keep her private life private. Or she would if she actually had a private life. Up until now, the most the media had been able to wring out of her was some vague speculation about who she might be dating, most often pairing her with Joe James or even Axle. They were going to have a field day with this.

"At least they don't know who he is," she murmured, more to herself than to Axle. Grant was an unknown. There would be some mild speculation, but it would quickly die down once he went back to Kentucky.

"Darling, aren't you listening? They know everything," Axle proclaimed, his tone ominous.

In her haste to turn it up, Vaughn fumbled the remote and dropped it before frantically searching the bed and locating it. She turned it up too much so that it blared and then readjusted it before it could wake Grant, sleeping in the next room.

"...Grant Honeywell, whose lawsuit claims that the book, *The Honeybear Chronicles,* is based on his life. He is suing Ms. Drake for defamation as well, though the suit doesn't seek any monetary reward. In an unusual move, he has instead requested a complete retraction and public apology. Although it appears from this picture that the two are intimate friends. I don't know, Charlie, what do you think?" The female "news" anchor turned to her cohost who answered her with a leering smile.

"Looks like a lover's quarrel gone wrong, don't you think, Janey? Although it's kind of cute that these two were high school sweethearts. *Celebrity Beat* has obtained exclusive high school photos of Vaughn Drake and let's just say there was more of her to love back then."

And then there they were, teenage pictures of Vaughn for all the world to see.

"Here's a picture of Vaughn with Grant Honeywell from that same yearbook," Charlie added as another picture popped up on the screen. This one was of Grant holding on to Vaughn while she frantically tried to get away, and instantly Vaughn remembered that moment. It was the last day of their junior year of high school, and they were having a field day to celebrate. There were water balloons, and Vaughn had been wearing a white t-shirt. For most of the day, she had avoided being hit, but then Grant captured her, drawing her into the contest so that she was pelted and soaked, making her white crisscross granny bra visible for all the world to see. She had never been able to wear pretty lingerie back then, having to wear ugly military-grade underwear to hold things in place.

"That's sweet," Janey said, smiling stupidly. At least Vaughn thought it looked stupid, and fake, too. Jane Keller hated her with a passion, something she knew for a fact. The woman was no doubt delighting in Vaughn's humiliation. Charlie Sanchez hated her, too. That was no doubt why the fat pictures from her adolescence remained on the screen for so long as the hosts pretended to ooze sympathy for Vaughn's unfortunate teenage years. "We'll definitely keep on top of this developing story."

Vaughn tossed herself onto her bed with a groan. She had been in the business long enough to understand that "We'll definitely keep on top of this developing story" was code for "This is the most fascinating thing to cross our desk today. We're going to hunt down everyone involved and prod the truth out of them or die trying. Goodbye to your private life, Vaughn Drake."

A polite tap sounded at her door. "Vaughn, everything okay in there?" Grant asked. "I heard noises."

"Come in," she told him.

He cracked the door and warily poked his head inside. Seeing that she was still sprawled in her bed, he opened the door wider. "You sick?"

"Sort of," she said. She pointed to the television where the show was once again rehashing pictures of her and Grant.

Grant walked in and plopped on the end of her bed, staring in shock at the television. "What is this?" he asked.

"Someone took our picture last night at Pink's." Belatedly she realized she had been on the phone to Axle at one point. She fished around in her bed for the forgotten phone, but of course he had hung up. Axle stayed on hold for no one.

"And they put it on the news?" Grant asked. "What's so exciting about a hot dog?"

"It's not the hot dog. It's us. They know everything." She flopped onto her back again, covering her eyes with her arm.

"This just happened a few hours ago. How could they know everything?" Grant asked.

"Because it's what they do. They're paid to mine these sorts of stories. The media is a huge machine with every tool at their disposal. They start with the internet, finding all the public information they can, and then they move on to people who know us."

"My family won't say anything," Grant said confidently.

"But people we went to high school with will, and probably already have if these pictures are any indication. My parents know better than to talk to anyone. But we graduated with a hundred and fifty other kids. One of them has probably dreamed of this moment." Her other arm joined the first, crisscrossing over her face as another groan escaped.

Grant leaned over her and smiled. "It's not so bad. So they took our picture and they found out we've known each other for a while. What's the big deal?" He peeled her arms away so he could see her face. He was like a Great Dane, she thought. All big, happy, sweet, and carefree. She envied him that attitude, and hoped the coming storm wouldn't douse it.

"You don't understand." She hadn't meant to whisper, but that was how it came out of her suddenly constricted throat as she realized that she was still in her pajamas and Grant Honeywell was in her bed, gently pinning her arms over her head.

"Explain it to me." Grant whispered, too, as his eyes flicked to her lips and lingered. Apparently the sudden tension in the room wasn't her imagination, and it wasn't one sided.

"We are now the biggest story in entertainment. They're going to do whatever it takes to catch us together, to photograph us every moment, to ferret information that will add to the drama."

"So I'll go home today," he said.

Her heart sank at that pronouncement, and that didn't make any sense at all. Wasn't that what she had wanted all along, for him to go away? "They'll follow you," she said. "They'll stake out your family's farm, sneaking around the barns to try and catch you off guard. They'll say things to you, horrible things that will make you angry, and then they'll take pictures of you when you respond."

"Why would they do that?"

"It's just how it works, but…" She broke off, hating to tell him the rest. "It will be worse because I'm involved."

"I don't understand," he said.

"They hate me," she said.

He rolled his eyes, smiling as he reached over to swipe a long strand of hair out of her eyes. "Vaughn, you think everyone hates you."

"No, I'm not making this up. They really, really hate me. I, uh, sort of used to be one of them."

He frowned now. "What do you mean?"

"Remember I said I wrote for a magazine in New York? I was a gossip columnist, a very good and very snarky one. I had a talent for finding people's secrets and outing them in a not-so-nice way. To say I made a lot of enemies would be putting it mildly."

Grant sighed and Vaughn resisted the urge to wince at the recrimination she read in his eyes. "Oh, Vaughn, what happened to you?"

It was the disappointment that brought the sudden rush of tears to her eyes. She turned her head to the side, not wanting him to see. "I got tired of being everyone's doormat, Grant," she whispered, and this time it was because her voice was choked with emotion. She glanced back up at him again, noting how his expression had softened. "I thought college would be so different, but it wasn't. I was still the fat cheerleader everyone thought it was okay to make fun of. And then I graduated and got a job working for the magazine as a copy editor, and it was more of the same. By this time, I had lost the weight, and I just didn't get it. I was skinny now; why were people still walking all over me? Then it was like a light bulb went off and I realized it was because I was letting them. So I stopped being a victim."

"And you started being a bully," he added, but gently this time.

"I guess it appears that way to you, but when people decide to live their lives in the public eye, then they make themselves open to gossip and ridicule." She quoted the mantra she had taught herself all those years ago when she was reporting on the private lives of celebrities. It was something she said often to make herself feel better.

"How's that working for you now?" Grant asked. "Does it feel good to be the center of the storm? To know there are hapless and innocent victims involved whose lives are going to be forever altered?"

She looked away again as the disappointment returned to his face. "Well I'm not doing it anymore, am I? I got out of that business."

"It seems to me that you simply traded talking about a bunch of strangers for talking about people you actually know," he said, and now he sounded angry again. He let her go, sitting up and leaning away from her. "I think it's better for everyone if I just go home and disappear."

Vaughn sat up. "Don't go home," she said. "Didn't you hear me? They'll follow you there and make your life a misery. Go somewhere secret, somewhere they can't find you. Do you have anywhere like that?"

He bit his lip, thinking. "I do." He glanced at her. "Do you?"

She shook her head. "It's too late for me, and I guess you're sort of right; I had this coming." She gave him a sheepish smile and he sighed, still staring at her.

"See, why did you have to go and turn humble all of a sudden? I could have left happily if you were still being a jerk. But now, I can't leave you like this alone and unprotected." He ran his hand through his hair. "You'll have to come with me."

"Come with you?" she repeated. "What are you talking about? I can't leave—I'm in the middle of shooting a movie."

"Vaughn, I can't leave you here in this mess, and I'm not staying. Can you imagine what people will say if they find out I slept in your house last night, what they'll think about us?"

Vaughn hopped out of bed and peeked through the slats in her window blinds. "That ship has sailed, Grant." She stood aside as he bent and peered through at the mass of paparazzi milling in front of the house. "By now they've run the tags on your rental car and know it belongs to you. They know you're in here, and they're waiting for us to come out."

He squinched his eyes closed and ran his hand through his hair again. "But nothing happened."

"Try telling that to them. Or don't because they won't listen. They've created a nice little story for us where we were high school sweethearts who broke up. I wrote my book out of heartbreak and despair, and you've come either to try and make amends or eke out your own revenge."

"Well that's sort of almost true," Grant said.

"Grant," Vaughn said, bonking his shoulder when she whirled to face him. "None of that is true. We weren't high school sweethearts."

"We were close," he said. "We would have been if you hadn't constantly run away from me. I swear half my life was wasted trying to pin you down, Vaughn."

She turned back to the window to avoid looking at him. "I wish you wouldn't say things like that."

"Like what? The truth? I had a blazing crush on you all through school, Vaughn, and you might as well know before the media finds out and blasts it all over the place. I wanted nothing more than to be your sweetheart."

Vaughn closed her eyes, wanting nothing more at that moment to believe him, to lean back on his broad chest and let him reassure her that, not only was everything going to be okay, but that his words were true, that she had been something special to him back then. Before she could give in to temptation, however, he continued speaking.

"Of course, that was then and this is now. I'm not sure we're the same people were then."

Vaughn knew that was his polite way of saying *she* wasn't the same. After all, hadn't he won least changed at their reunion? While she had apparently become a bitter, fame-seeking harpy, at least in his mind. Or maybe in reality. Who knew anymore what was true? Sometimes

Vaughn had no idea who she really was. How could she expect him to know?

He lightly touched her waist, giving it a squeeze that made her jump. "Pack your bags. I'm taking you away from here."

She shook her head, but it was too late; he was already gone.

CHAPTER 9

"Axle, I'm being kidnapped."

"Darling, what's going on? Is it one of the Paps?"

"No, it's not the paparazzi; it's Grant. He's forcing me to go away with him."

Axle chuckled. "Sounds delightful."

"It's not," Vaughn said, frustrated. Axle was supposed to be on her side. He was supposed to help. "I'm in the middle of shooting a movie. I can't go away to wherever I'm going."

"Look, darling, it's Thursday. So what if you miss a couple days of shooting? It's not like you're one of the actors. They can get by without you. Go away for your little weekend, and come back refreshed. You deserve a break anyway."

"This isn't a little weekend, and it's not fun," Vaughn said. "He's taking me away from the media because he thinks it's the best thing for me."

"Taking you away from the media?" Axle repeated, sounding alarmed now. As a publicist, being away from the media spotlight was akin to being dead. "Don't go."

She rolled her eyes. "That's what I've been trying to tell you. He's not giving me a choice." She glared at Grant who was ignoring her as if she wasn't even there. He had stuffed her into her car in the garage, opened the door, and barreled through the paparazzi, not even pausing when a couple of them rolled off the hood.

"Good thing you have an SUV," had been his only comment for the last hour as they headed who knew where.

"Where is he taking you?" Axle asked.

"I don't know," Vaughn said. "He won't tell me."

Axle let out a breath. "Leave this to me, darling. I'll put out a press release and spin this in our direction. I'll make this work."

"I don't care about making it work, Axle, I want to go home. I want to get out of here, wherever here is."

"What can I do, darling?"

His tone was more helpless than caring, and Vaughn sighed. "Nothing. I just wanted to vent."

"All right. Keep me updated, darling." She could tell he was smiling, and that annoyed her, and so did all the "darlings." She and Axle had started out together on the east coast when he was still Bernie. Why did he insist on keeping up the charade with her when she knew the truth of who he was?

"Is Alex going to ride in on his fake British horse and save you?" Grant asked as she closed the phone and tossed it on the floor.

"It's Axle."

"No, it's *Bernie*. No wonder the poor guy took a pseudonym. Who does that to their child?"

"I don't know. Who names their child *Corliss*?"

He pressed his lips together at the mention of his brother. "That's a family name," he said.

"Maybe Bernie is, too."

"I suppose." He sighed. "Sorry, I'm just hungry. I get cranky when I'm hungry."

Tell me about it—I've been both hungry and cranky for eight years. She didn't say that, though. It would only add fuel to the fire he had built against her diet. He pulled into the first restaurant he saw, a greasy spoon that didn't look safe.

"This is a dive," she said.

"Sometimes dives have the best food."

"Sometimes dives have botulism," she replied.

Grant laughed. "You are wound tighter than a tangled fishing reel," he said as he opened her door. Vaughn hadn't realized she had been waiting for him to do so until it was over. Odd how old habits returned. She wasn't sure she had waited on a man to open a door for her in years. Then again she hadn't had a date in years. Grant grasped her hand to help her down from the SUV, though she was perfectly tall enough to reach the ground on her own. "Relax," he added, giving her hand a small shake.

Her response was automatic as she inhaled and exhaled, trying to release some of her tension, and then her frustration and anxiety returned with a vengeance. She snatched her hand from his. "How am I supposed to relax when I'm being kidnapped and forced to eat at Mel's diner?" She frowned at the dilapidated restaurant. It wasn't actually called Mel's, but it reminded her of the diner from the old TV show.

"You know what your problem is, Vaughn?" Grant said, his angry expression telling her that she had upset him.

"I'm going to go out on a limb here and guess that you're going to tell me," Vaughn said.

"You don't know what's good for you," Grant said. "You don't let yourself indulge in anything that will make your life better like food, sleep, days off, or friends."

"I have friends," she said.

"Name one," he dared.

"Axle," she replied.

"An axle it not a friend; it's the thing that keeps the car together. Name another."

She searched her mind and came up blank. "What about you? Who are your friends? Someone not in your immediate family," she added.

"You're going to meet one in a little while," he said. He didn't add "so there," but she could tell by his smug expression he wanted to. "And since we're on this road trip together, you might try being pleasant for once, just to make life bearable for those around you."

Her mouth opened in injured surprise. "I am not unpleasant."

"Prove it." He turned her toward the ramshackle eating establishment. "Go in there, order off the menu, eat it, and don't complain about anything."

Vaughn shook free of his clutch, proudly tipping her head up as she walked toward the dreaded diner. *I can do this,* she told herself. *It's just food. How bad can it be?*

It turned out the answer was "Very." It was dirty and deserted. Vaughn and Grant were the only people there, a bad sign if there ever was one. Still, she scanned the menu, hopeful to find one thing she could eat. Her hope turned to dismay at the abundance of things fried or covered in gravy. *This is California, for goodness sake. Haven't these people heard of the health food movement?* She kept her comments to herself, mentally stewing as she added up possible calorie consumption in her head. At last she decided on the vegetable soup while Grant ordered the special, some meatloaf concoction.

When her soup arrived, it was swimming in grease, but she bravely battled on, searching through the swampy mess for the promised vegetables. What she found instead were pieces of what looked like fish. Swallowing against her gag reflex, she loaded up her spoon, closed her eyes, and opened her mouth, but that was as far as she got. Her eyes popped open in surprise as Grant's hand clamped on hers. He shook his head at her before picking up his napkin to spit something into it.

"I don't know what that was, but it wasn't beef. Whatever you do, don't eat anything here." He stood, pulled some bills from his wallet, and tossed them on the table, still grimacing as he waited for Vaughn to follow him to the car. To her surprise, he draped his arm on her shoulders as they walked outside.

"You were right about that place. That was a horrible choice. Sorry," he said, giving her shoulders a light squeeze before dropping his arm.

Vaughn blinked at him. Was he for real? Did a man just admit to her that he was wrong and then apologize?

"No big deal," Vaughn said, drawing out the words as she tried to figure him out. What was his angle? Did he want something from her? Was this a trick to get her to lower her defenses and trust him so he could turn around and stab her in the back? If so, he was a master manipulator because it was beginning to work.

Grant opened the car door for her and remained standing beside her after she sat down. "You were really going to eat it, weren't you?"

She nodded, hiding her shudder at how close she had come to consuming whatever had been in that bowl. He smiled, a genuine smile that somehow conveyed his pleasure at her actions and, like the desperate teenager she had once been, she found herself smiling almost shyly in return. "Thatta girl," he said, and she found herself wondering what she could do to earn his approval again.

With the slamming of the car door, though, came some semblance of sanity. What was she doing acting like a love-struck teenager with this man? They weren't seventeen anymore. And when they had been seventeen, he had hurt and humiliated her. One smile and she was willing to forget all her hard-earned lessons. Men were not to be trusted, and especially not this man.

Grant poked her leg, shaking her out of her gloomy thoughts. "Why don't you find the next restaurant for us on your fancy phone?"

Dutifully, she picked up her phone and began scrolling through local options until she located a café in the upcoming town. It had good ratings and, best of all, it looked at least halfway healthy.

"This looks sort of girly," Grant said when they pulled up in front.

"You might try being pleasant for once, just to make life bearable for those around you." She imitated his deep voice, affecting her long-dormant accent as she threw his words back in his face.

"I can't believe you've let your accent go when it's so cute," he said.

"How can you even hear it?" she asked. "Don't I sound like everyone else back home?"

"I guess maybe it stands out more because you so rarely use it. Now, pray tell me, what is so bad about our accent that you felt the need to give it up?"

"People treat you like you're stupid when you have a southern accent, especially when you're a woman," she informed him. "This industry is competitive, and I needed every advantage I could get."

"Did it ever occur to you that your accent could be an advantage?" he said. "It's charming, Vaughn, and it's part of who you are. Why not embrace it and play it up?"

"No offense, Grant, but I'm not really looking to take career advice from a farmer."

"Oh, how could I possibly be offended by that?" He rolled his eyes. "And, for the record, I wasn't offering career advice; that was life advice."

"Well, then, let me just get out my journal and write that down. I'll start a new entry—life advice by Grant Honeywell. How to earn a degree in engineering and waste it will be the subtitle."

"At least I'm happy," he said. "Are you?"

"I thought you said you were hungry," she pointed out.

In response, he reached across the seat and unfastened her safety belt. "You just had that entire conversation without dropping your accent. I think I'm having a good effect on you."

"You're not having any effect on me at all," she said, lying through her teeth as his hand lingered near her hip.

"Some things never change," Grant said. He removed his hand, came around to retrieve her, and they went inside to eat.

CHAPTER 10

*a*fter breakfast, Vaughn fell asleep. When she woke again, several hours later, they had arrived at their destination.

"Where are we?" she asked, staring at a brick house with green shutters that screamed "post war development."

"In Sacramento at my friend's house. We went to college together."

His tone was strained. She looked up and noticed he was pale and sweating profusely. "Are you okay?"

He nodded once, curtly, and opened his door, holding tight to the handle as he hopped down. Vaughn kept an eye on him as he unloaded their bags from the back, his lips tightly pressed together.

"Need any help?" she asked.

He resolutely shook his head, not saying a word. Before she could press him to tell her what was wrong, however, they were standing on the front porch and ringing the doorbell. Vaughn wasn't sure what to expect, but she was still surprised by the sight of the small Asian woman who opened the door, an excited smile lighting her face.

"Grant!" she exclaimed, launching herself at him. Grant returned her hug, pulling her in tight and enveloping her tiny frame in his massive arms. That was when Vaughn realized that the bitter taste on the back of her tongue was jealousy. Who was this woman and, more importantly, who was she to Grant?

The woman stepped back and looked up at Vaughn—way up. "This is Vaughn," Grant said.

The woman's mouth puckered slightly in a silent "O" of surprise. "Vaughn," she repeated the name as if it held some significance for her.

"And this is China," Grant finished the introductions.

Vaughn's eyes narrowed on the woman. "But you're Korean."

Once again, she had taken the woman by surprise. "Most people can't tell the difference," China said. "Ten points for Gryffindor."

Grant's index finger scratched his temple as he turned almost apologetically to Vaughn. "She always says stuff like that. I never have any idea what she's talking about."

Vaughn and China exchanged a smile and a look. The smile seemed to say "Isn't he adorable?" while the look said, "Who are you to him?"

"Are you an engineer?" Vaughn asked as China moved aside to grant them entrance.

"Software engineer," China explained. "I develop video games."

"So you guys had classes together in college," Vaughn said, trying to draw the other woman out. Had they dated? The woman was cute but short with a boyish figure, certainly not at all Grant's ideal, or at least according to him.

"Yep," China replied. Either she was being purposely evasive, or she had no idea that Vaughn was trying to get to the bottom of their relationship. "Here you go." She paused in front of a small, plain guest room, almost daring Vaughn to comment on the drab little space.

"Thank you for taking us in like this," Vaughn said, being careful to sound perfectly polite. She had no idea what Grant had told her about the situation. Had they talked while Vaughn was sleeping? If so, she hadn't heard them.

"I would do anything for this big lug," China said, patting Grant's bicep.

He smiled down at her and, despite the sheen of sweat on his forehead, the smile was warm and sincere. "Let me show you to your room," China added to Grant who followed her from the room as Vaughn watched, fighting down another wave of jealousy. She sat on her bed, staring through the door and down the hall. The house was small enough that she could make out the murmur of voices, but not so small that she could tell what they were saying. Were they talking about her? But then the voices stopped and a new, more horrifying possibility occurred to her. Were they kissing?

But then China walked back down the hallway, Grant-less. A minute later Vaughn heard Grant enter the bathroom, which was apparently right next door to her room because she could hear everything, and from the sounds, Grant was horribly sick.

She stood up, alarm and uncertainty fighting for supremacy. Should she go to him and try to help? Or should she stay here and wait until he was finished? In the end, she walked to the bathroom, tapping softly on the door.

"Grant," she said. "Are you okay?"

He groaned in reply.

She didn't want to do this. She wasn't good with sick people. Still, Grant was sort of her responsibility. Steeling herself, she opened the door and peeked in, just in time to see Grant heave violently into the commode.

"Go away, Vaughn," he gasped as soon as he realized she was there. "You don't want to see this."

No, I don't, she thought. But there was something sad about being sick and alone so far from home. She knew because it had happened to her more times than she could count. And every time she was sick, she wished for someone to come and take care of her. With that bracing thought in mind, she stepped forward and ran a soothing hand over Grant's back.

"Done?" she asked.

"For now," he said.

She closed the lid and flushed before pushing him to a sitting position on the commode. To her surprise, he sank down weakly and then pressed the top of his head to the soft spot on her stomach, the one she couldn't seem to tone no matter how many crunches she did.

"Go away," he repeated again. "This is gross." Still, despite his words, his arms snaked around her and clung. She smiled as she petted the top of his head. Maybe it was true all men turned into little boys when they were sick. "I haven't thrown up since I was five. We Honeywells pride ourselves on never getting sick."

"What don't you Honeywells pride yourself on?" she asked.

"Showing weakness in front of a woman," he said, and then he roughly shoved her away before dashing to his feet, throwing open the lid, and heaving again.

Vaughn squeezed her eyes shut and held her breath as she gently rubbed his back again. She had no idea if that was actually helping, but it was what her mother had done for her whenever she was sick, and it had always felt good, even if because it was some form of human contact in the midst of abject misery.

Grant finished again and flushed, resuming his seat on the closed toilet lid. "This is horrible, honey. Please go away." The request lost some meaning when he pressed his face to her stomach, his arms clinging tight. The endearment caught her off guard, but then she remembered in their part of Kentucky endearments were practically taught as parts of speech. His hair was soaked with sweat, and he was trembling violently, causing Vaughn's heart to wrench in pity. There was something truly awful about seeing such a large capable man so ill.

She eased out of his embrace and left the bathroom. Heading to her room to remove the cover from the bed, she returned and wrapped it around Grant's shoulders. His expression at her return was a mixture of hope and helplessness. "You should stay away," he said. "Leave me."

She smiled, retrieving a washcloth from the basket on the counter. She soaked it in cold water and bathed his face. "You make it sound like you're dying."

"I truly think maybe I am," he said, tipping his face up to her as she swiped his forehead with the cool cloth.

Vaughn laughed. "Not on my watch, sugar," she said, then she bent and bestowed a kiss on his clammy forehead.

&a,

A few hours later, Vaughn thought maybe it was over. She sat on the floor of the small bathroom, Grant folded up into a pretzel, his head resting in her lap as he—finally, thankfully—slept. The washcloth was still pressed to his forehead and Vaughn ran her fingers through his hair, over and over again with the irrational fear that if she stopped he might wake up and get sick again.

China poked her head in, as she had been doing all evening. She nodded in approval when she saw that Grant was sleeping. "Can I get you anything?" she asked Vaughn.

"No thanks," Vaughn replied, hoping her whisper would give the other woman a hint that she was being too loud.

"It's okay," China replied. "Once he's out, he's out. Nothing can wake him."

And you know this because... Vaughn stared at her, the words on the tip of her tongue. Apparently China thought Vaughn's vigil had earned an answer because she continued speaking.

"We used to study together. Grant sometimes fell asleep and then he was stuck wherever he was for the night because he was impossible to wake. It was inconvenient when it happened at a restaurant or in the lobby of my dorm."

"He really slept all night in a restaurant?" Vaughn asked, not bothering to whisper anymore.

China nodded. "More than once. And of course I never had enough money to keep us there all night, so I would have to raid his wallet to pay for endless coffee and muffins. Talk about awkward. I always felt like I was robbing him, but of course he didn't care. He would wake up at exactly six AM, fresh as a daisy and sheepish about having fallen asleep. I bet you anything that he'll wake up at six tomorrow morning. It's like the time has been programmed into his brain." She smiled lovingly at Grant.

"What was he like in college?" Vaughn asked.

China sat cross legged just outside the bathroom door. "Sweet. Shy. It was unreal, you know? We were in the middle of party central, like an extended beer-induced episode of *Girls Gone Wild,* and there was Grant—wholesome, honest, and sober. And yet people loved him."

"He told me he didn't have many friends," Vaughn said.

"Probably not by his definition. He's friendly, but he doesn't let many people get close. There weren't a lot of trustworthy candidates back then. Everyone seemed more concerned with having a good time than developing deep connections."

"How long did you guys date?" There, it was out, the question Vaughn had been dying to ask.

China laughed. "In my dreams? For a very long time. In reality, not at all. I was interested, but he wasn't. He's always treated me like a sister. Eventually I gave up hope and moved on, but it took a really long time to stop comparing everyone to Grant. He's just so..." She paused and looked Vaughn directly in the eye. "If I were you, I'd never let him go."

"We're not together," Vaughn said. "In fact, I don't think he likes me very much."

Grant was doing his best to prove her wrong as he shifted position and tossed his arm around her waist, hugging her closer like a human teddy bear.

"He told me about you," China said as if confessing a horrible secret. "He didn't talk about himself much, but this one night we were sick and tired of studying, and we ended up talking for hours."

"What, uh," Vaughn began, then paused and cleared her throat, trying to tamp down her eagerness, "what did he say about me?"

China's eyes rested on Grant, trying to determine if she should answer. "It's not so much what he said as what he didn't say. He told me a story about meeting you in kindergarten. He said you were almost as tall as him and he thought you were pretty so he pulled your hair. And you pulled his right back. I think he thought that was pretty great. And then it was like the cork had been pulled and all these stories poured out with you as the central character. It was pretty obvious you're his dream woman."

"That's the problem," Vaughn said, gazing down at Grant's peaceful face. "He sees me as something I'm not, something I've never been. And he likes me better fat." She glanced up at China, as perplexed by that statement as she was by the fact that she was sharing it. She wasn't one for making female friends easily.

China laughed. "That sounds about right. He's not quite normal. What are his brothers like? I never met them."

"Mythical," Vaughn breathed in the awed tone one used when speaking of the Honeywell Pack. "If you don't know them, they all look exactly alike. They're kind of the peacekeepers of our town, you know? I mean, we have a police force, but everyone knows that if you misbehave, the Honeywells will find a way to correct you. But they're also really generous. They secretly pay for things like building repairs and holiday celebrations. Everyone knows it's them, but no one talks about it. Some people resent them for their wealth and power. Some people think they're nothing more than thugs with money." She swallowed down a sudden lump of guilt. "And I probably just made things worse for them. I sort of wrote a book about them, about Grant."

"What is it?" China asked.

"*The Honeybear Chronicles.*"

China's jaw dropped. "That was you? Grant is Grady Honeybear?" Her eyes fell on Grant again, frowning in confusion. "But Grady was so mean, and that's not Grant at all. He's one of the sweetest most genuine people I've ever met. Has he changed that much since high school?"

"I don't know," Vaughn said, and to her dismay she sounded as if she was about to cry. "He says he didn't do any of that stuff, but I was there. How could I have gotten it so wrong? He crushed me, or so I thought."

China shook her head. "I'm telling you, Vaughn, Grant would never purposely hurt anyone. If he says he didn't do it, then he didn't do it."

There was a part of Vaughn that didn't want to believe her

because, if she did, then *she* was the bad guy in this scenario. She had written a book and was now making a movie based on lies, lies about the man whose face was now in her lap. Her hard-earned vindication would instead be an unprovoked attack on an innocent man, and she couldn't live with that. "There's no way to undo what I've done. He's never going to forgive me."

"Of course he will," China assured her. "He's Grant. You could probably punch him in the face, and he would laugh about it."

"I'm not sure about that. Sometimes I think he hates me." She sounded pathetic; she felt pathetic.

"If I knew the secret to capturing Grant's heart, I would have used it long ago," China said. "But I do know that he values honesty, integrity, and good character. Beyond that, what he wants in a woman is elusive. I'm not even sure he knows. He's not one given to deep thought."

They were silent a few minutes, both staring at Grant. It was strange having nothing else in common with this woman but the guy on the floor, the guy who had been out of her life for the last ten years before coming back into it with a vengeance.

"Are you going to stay here all night?" China asked.

"According to you I don't have much chance of waking him so, yes, I guess I am."

"Want a pillow?"

"That would be great," Vaughn said, smiling.

China left and returned a few seconds later with a pillow and another blanket. "I'm not sure I've ever been so jealous of someone who's so uncomfortable before," she said as she handed Vaughn the items.

"I'm not sure there's much to be jealous of," Vaughn said.

"I wouldn't be too sure about that," China said. "I saw the way he looked at you when he introduced me."

"How did he look at me?" Vaughn asked, unable to control the blatant hope and longing in her tone.

"The way he's never looked at me," China said. Her smile looked a little melancholy as she turned and left the bathroom.

CHAPTER 11

Vaughn woke with her head resting on the thin edge of the bathroom door, her neck bent at an impossible angle so that when she opened her eyes, she was looking squarely at Grant who was looking back at her. And smiling.

"Feeling better?" she asked, using the question as an excuse to smooth her hand over his forehead, checking for clamminess.

"Yes," he said. "I'm sorry about that, sorry you had to deal with that. I never..."

She interrupted him. "You never get sick; I know."

"I was going to say I never let anyone see me get sick. Not since I was a kid, not since my mom." He winced. "Not that I'm comparing you to my mom," he hastened to add.

"What? I'm not good enough to be compared to your mom?"

"No, I didn't, I mean..."

Now it was her turn to cut him off with a laugh. "I'm just messing with you."

He smiled again, looking relieved. That sat there for a few beats in silence that felt more companionable than heavy, but Vaughn supposed this was their version of a foxhole experience. Watching a person empty his stomach of its contents was a definite bonding incident, if not a fun one. Absently, she continued running her hand over his forehead and through his hair.

"I didn't take you for a touchy-feely person," Grant commented at last.

Vaughn froze with her fingers in his hair, suddenly self-conscious. "Sorry, does it bother you?"

"Of course not," he said. "We Honeywells, we're tactile. I, uh, I like it. A lot."

His forehead was definitely warm now, probably because he was blushing. He must be the only twenty eight year old man on the planet who blushed at the thought of being touched by a woman. After living on her own for so many years in the big city, Vaughn should probably find that odd. Maybe she would if they had just met, but she knew where he came from, knew how conservative his family was, and instead she found his conventional attitudes charming.

"I like it, too," Vaughn surprised them both with the admission. She *was* a touchy-feely person, but she was also standoffish and distrustful. These days the only people she touched were her parents when she hugged them hello and goodbye. It was nice to have a legitimate reason to reach out and touch someone, and it was as comforting to her as it—hopefully—was to him.

"What time is it?" he asked. He closed his eyes again, sounding relaxed as she kept up the gentle ritual of running her fingers through his hair.

She looked up at the clock on the opposite wall, squinting. "Just a little after six," she said, smiling.

He opened his eyes again. "What's funny?"

"China said you have an internal alarm clock and always wake at six."

"I do?" he asked, sounding surprised.

"Don't you know what time you wake up?"

"I never gave it much thought before, but I guess it is always six when I look at the clock." He shook his head. "That's amazing."

"The fact that you've lived twenty eight years without realizing something so monumental about yourself?"

"Nah, that happens to me all the time. I meant it's amazing China would remember my wakeup time after all these years. She must have a good memory for quirky things."

Or she was and still is totally in love with you. She would have said it, but the house was small. She couldn't be sure China wasn't listening, and she didn't want to be rude by outing her secret. "Why did you guys never date?" she asked instead.

"I don't think she's ever been interested in me that way," Grant said. Vaughn laughed, but he sounded completely serious.

"Grant, you can't possibly be that obtuse," she said, lowering her voice to a whisper.

"What are you talking about?" he asked.

She leaned closer to make sure what she was about to say wouldn't be overheard. "I'm talking about the fact that the woman probably had 'China Honeywell' written all over every notebook she ever had in college."

Grant laughed. "You're messing with me again," he accused.

"I'm not. She was over the moon about you; she still is."

He looked so shell-shocked by that information that Vaughn began kicking herself. "Do you, uh, still like her that way?" she added, twirling a lock of his freakishly thick hair around her index finger.

"Vaughn, come on," Grant said. "Don't be crazy."

What did that mean? *Don't be crazy—of course I'm still in love with her.* Or maybe, *Don't be crazy; how could I be in love with her when I'm in love with you?* Right. That one was likely.

"Why is it crazy? You two obviously have a history together and you're good friends. Isn't a good friendship the best basis for romance?" Vaughn asked.

He sat up and moved away from her. "Do you want me to date her?"

"What is it to me?" she asked.

He looked at her, his expression darkening to a frown as she squirmed uncomfortably and looked away. "Nothing at all, apparently." He stood, trying to hide the fact that he swayed slightly. "If you don't mind vacating the bathroom, I'm going to shower and scrub my teeth a few dozen times."

She stood, hating the fact that she had once again ruined the moment. What was wrong with her? Was she secretly bent on self-sabotage? "No problem," she lied. She wanted to flee to her room, fling herself across the bed, and have a good cry. Instead she forced herself to turn and look at him. "Can I get you anything? Juice? Toast?"

He shook his head. Grimacing. "Food still doesn't sound good. Maybe after I shower. Thanks." He held her eyes for just a second before turning away, dismissing her.

She plodded back to her room and crawled on top of the bed full clothed, coverless because it remained in the bathroom with Grant. It didn't matter, though. She was so exhausted and frazzled that the second she closed her eyes, she was asleep.

❦

"Vaughn."

Someone was whispering, very close to her face.

"Mmm," she grunted, rolling over to block them out.

"Vaughn." The whisper was more persistent, and it was joined by a hand on her shoulder. The hand began shaking her.

She repeated her earlier "mmm," adding in more anger this time to let the whisperer feel her ire. She was nowhere near ready to be conscious.

"Vaughn, sweetheart, wake *up!*"

Now two hands were on her shoulders, and they were jostling her so that she bounced up and down on the bed, but it was the whispered "sweetheart" that finally roused her. "Grant?" she murmured, confused.

He let go her shoulders, bracing his hands on either side of her face. And he was smiling as he leaned over her. "Morning, sleepyhead," he said, sounding perfectly cheerful.

"Weren't we arguing?" she blurted.

"I don't remember. I've never been very good at staying angry. But, if you want, I could try." He pretended to scowl at her, and she laughed, changing his fake scowl to a genuine smile.

"No, I think I prefer it this way. It's like dating an amnesiac." She pressed her lips together before scrambling to continue. "I mean, not that I think we're dating. You know what I mean, I just…" Oh, geez, were these babbling sounds really coming out of her mouth? Wasn't she supposed to be a writer and good with words?

"I'm starting to remember why I was mad at you," Grant said. With a sigh, he pushed away from her and sat up straight. "I'm sorry to wake you, but the photographers found us. They're here."

"Here?" she asked, her eyes darting frantically around the room.

Grant laughed. "You don't exactly wake up coherent, do you? Yes, Vaughn, they're in this very room. I thought it would be a good idea to bring them along when I woke you up."

"Sarcasm doesn't suit you, Grant," she said.

He grinned. "I know. I could never pull it off. You should hear my brother, Everett, do it, though. He's like a grand champion. Anyway, we should probably go soon if we're going to try and evade them. China and I have been hashing out a plan."

Now she began to remember why they had been fighting. *China.* What else had they been hashing out? Their missed opportunity for romance in college?

"You probably have time for a shower if you hurry. I packed some food so you can eat in the car. Skip the hair and makeup routine, if you don't mind. We don't have time." He reached up and lightly brushed his fingers against her temple, pushing a lock of hair off her face. "You may not wake up coherent, but you sure wake up pretty, Vaughn."

And then he was gone, just like that, and Vaughn discovered he wasn't the only twenty eight year old on the planet who still blushed.

CHAPTER 12

"Well that was fun," Grant said, smiling like he meant it, which he probably did.

Vaughn refrained from saying what she was thinking, which was *You're not right in the head, Grant.* After all, he was still pale, sweaty and shaky. Despite the fact that he hadn't gotten sick for the last few hours, she knew he wasn't back to a hundred percent. Maybe illness accounted for why he thought being pursued by a pack of paparazzi was somehow fun.

"We could have died," Vaughn was unable to resist saying. "Like Princess Di."

He glanced at her, smiling. "You really think I would let you die, Vaughn?"

It was on the tip of her tongue to sarcastically suggest that he thought he was Superman, but she held back. He actually did look a little like Superman with his extreme build and thick black hair. In fact, it was uncanny how much of the time he acted like Clark Kent. But if Vaughn was being honest, she would admit she hadn't felt like they were in danger. Instead what she had actually felt was jealousy, and how embarrassing was that?

Sitting at China's kitchen table a little while ago, watching them plot and plan, their heads close together, Vaughn had thought she couldn't possibly get any more jealous. And then she realized that part of the plan included using China as a decoy. Apparently Grant was really impressed by her bravery and selflessness. Vaughn knew because he said so—repeatedly.

He had hugged China goodbye as if she were a soldier being sent to the front lines, and then they had watched while she jumped in her car and barreled from the garage, a large number of paparazzi on her tail. Then Grant had grabbed Vaughn's hand, hustled her into the car, and taken off in another direction while the remaining photographers were still struggling to get into their vehicles. It wasn't a foolproof plan because there had still been four cars on their tail, but Grant had lost them through a series of death-defying maneuvers that he had apparently found *fun.*

"I hope China's okay," he said now, bringing Vaughn's simmering jealousy back to the surface. "How do you think the photographers found us there?"

"Let's see, who knew we were there? Me, you, and China. We were both busy all night. Who does that leave?"

"Vaughn," Grant said, shooting her a disparaging look before returning his eyes to the road. "China wouldn't do that. What a terrible thing to say about one of my friends, and one who just put us up for the night, no less."

Vaughn refused to give in to her twinge of conscience. Of course she didn't actually think China had ratted them out, but there was no good way to explain her comment without revealing her jealousy. And so she forged on, making things worse. "You'd be surprised by what fame can do to some people, Grant."

"No, I'm not sure I would," Grant said.

Vaughn frowned. Obviously he was talking about her. Or was he?

"But I do know China, and she would never do that to me, or even to you," Grant said. "Besides, I thought you liked her. It seemed like you guys bonded or something."

"She's all right," Vaughn said. In truth, she had liked China very much. But that did nothing to tamp her insatiable curiosity over what was between Grant and the pretty little engineer. They had so much in common and China was so *nice*, nice in the way that Grant had once thought Vaughn was nice, nice in the way he admired. She had none of Vaughn's snarkiness or cynicism. And it was obvious that she adored Grant.

"Maybe it was Bernie," Grant said.

"What?" Vaughn asked, tearing her distracted gaze from the window to stare at him.

"Your publicist friend strikes me as the kind to rat you out," Grant said.

"He would not. And, besides, he didn't even know where we were. I haven't talked to him since we left yesterday." Which was kind of odd, really. Usually she and Axle talked every day, if not more than once. Why hadn't he called? What was the world saying about them? Was it so bad that Axle didn't want to tell her?

"What's between you two anyway?" Grant asked. "My sister-in-law, Haley, showed me a picture of you two, and it said he's your on-again, off-again boyfriend, and I really hope that's not true, Vaughn, because that guy is a snake."

"So I'm not allowed to say things about your sainted friends, but you're allowed to say things about mine?"

"Yes because what I'm saying is true," Grant said.

"It is not," Vaughn said.

"Which part? The part about him being a snake, or the part about him being your boyfriend?" Grant asked, and he was almost yelling now.

Vaughn turned her head to the window, refusing to answer. Grant took a deep breath and let it out slowly. "I'm sorry. I didn't mean to get so angry, but I really don't get it. What do you see in that guy?"

His apologetic tone evaporated her anger, and she found herself really wanting to explain things to him. "He and I, we're kindred spirits."

Grant's expression was of someone who had just sucked on a lemon. "No way."

Vaughn chuckled. "I'm serious. You didn't know him when he was

Bernie. He was sweet and innocent in a business that eats the sweet and innocent for breakfast. He worked for a publicist in New York, and I was a lowly copy editor for the magazine. We met at a party because we were both at the edge of the room, trying to blend into the woodwork. This is probably hard for you to believe because he looks so smooth and sophisticated now, but he was poorly dressed and rail thin back then, with bad hair and bad teeth, too."

"That's not hard for me to believe at all," Grant interrupted, but Vaughn ignored him.

"And so we formed this bond, the unbreakable band of losers, you might say. He started feeding me information about clients at his firm, and I used it to work my way up the ladder at the magazine. Before I knew it, I was a full-fledged writer, and then it was my turn to help Axle. My star began to rise, and I dragged him up with me. He returned the favor. We had a good thing going with him feeding me all the news I wanted while I reported on his clients, making them even more famous so he got even more work."

"And then what happened?" Grant asked, sensing that there was a "but" coming.

"And then my book got published and rocketed to number one. Apparently being picked on in high school is a resounding theme. You can't believe the letters I get." She paused, shaking her head. "There are some real jerks out there."

"Speaking of Bernie, what happened to him after you got famous?" Grant asked.

"He moved to the west coast and started his own business. He's just…he's one of those people that I can be myself with. There's no judgment, you know? He doesn't judge me for being the former fat girl, or for being the famous author, or for being a gossip columnist. It's all just the same to him. He likes me for me." She turned to look out the window again, wishing they weren't trapped in the car together. Grant was quiet, but it was a thoughtful silence. As if on cue, Vaughn's phone rang, and it was Axle.

"Hello, darling, where are you?"

"I have no idea," Vaughn said wearily.

"Are you all right? Do you need me to call the police or what not?"

"No, I'm fine. I'm just tired. I didn't get much sleep last night."

"Yes, I know. I saw it on the news."

Vaughn frowned, resisting the urge to pull the phone away from her ear and look at it. Was it possible that Axle sounded jealous? Of her and Grant? "What are they saying?"

"That you stayed the night together at a house in Sacramento."

While that was factually true, the innuendo in his tone was nowhere near the truth. "That's not how it was, Axle. You have to tell them that."

He laughed, a short humorless chuckle. "Vaughn, darling, you know that won't do any good. They've set you two up as some sort of romantic duo, and there's nothing that will change it. This is possibly the biggest story I've ever handled, and it has snowballed way out of my control."

She sighed, pinching the bridge of her nose. "Do you have any idea how they found us?"

"None whatsoever," he said. "But you know how it is. They have their ways. You used to be very talented at finding people who wished to stay hidden."

"Yeah, I guess I did," she said. She lowered her voice, turning her back to Grant so she could whisper into the phone. "Axle, I think I might be a truly horrible person." She wanted him to contradict her, but he laughed again.

"Of course you are, darling, and that's why I love you. Take care now, love, and keep me updated." And just like that, he was gone.

She sat clutching the silent phone and willing herself not to cry. She should be on the top of the world right now with a book on the bestseller list, a movie being made, money in the bank, her excess fat finally banished. But she didn't feel happy; she felt empty and alone. Axle thought she was a bad person? He knew her better than anyone, and he truly thought she was a bad person.

Grant reached over and snatched her phone, tucking it into her purse. "As long as we have so much time on our hands, let's talk about the book."

Just like that Vaughn's self-pity and self-loathing disappeared because remembering the book made her remember why she wrote it in the first place, and that made her remember Grant and all the mistreatment she had suffered at his hands.

"Fine. Let's talk about the book," she said, flinging out the words as though they were a challenge.

"Let me preface by saying that I understand now that high school wasn't all rainbows and sunshine for you," he said. His tone was that of someone who was dealing with a mentally ill person who was off her meds, and when Vaughn snorted in disgust, he looked even warier. "Some kids were mean to you; I get that now. But what I don't understand is why you felt the need to make up all that stuff about me. What did I ever do to you?"

"Everything that's in the book," Vaughn said, exasperated beyond reason. "Look, I've come to understand that you're an honest person, Grant, so I don't understand why you won't just admit this. Just say, 'Yes, I was an immature jerk in high school, and I did some horrible things to you. For that I'm sorry, but I've grown.' That's all I want—an admission and an apology. But you won't even admit it. You act like you weren't there, like none of it even happened when I know it did." Her tone was rising in volume and intensity because he was shaking his head violently back and forth.

"No. No way. I would never, ever, ever have done any of that stuff to you, Vaughn. I already admitted I had a huge, raging inferno of a crush on you. Why would I have picked on you?"

Vaughn covered her eyes with her hand, fighting a headache. "I don't know, Grant. All I know is what I experienced. I know it was real, and I know it was you."

"Give me an example."

Her mind flashed to the fateful party, but she still couldn't go there. The memory was still too fresh, still too painful. "Let's start with your little nickname for me."

He shifted uncomfortably in his seat. "You knew about that?"

"Of course I knew. You don't think every cheerleader on my squad wasn't dying to tell me that the most sought after guy in school labeled me the Amazon?" Her heart sank because he hadn't denied it; he had really called her that horrible, hurtful name.

"Okay, I said it, but it was supposed to be a compliment."

She snorted. "Are you kidding me? How is a name like 'Amazon' supposed to be a compliment to a girl who is almost six feet tall and overweight?"

"Okay, here's what happened," he said, shifting again. "I was watching you run cross country, which I did often because, like I said, I was a little obsessed. So I'm watching you run, and I was with Corby who had no idea I was there to watch you because I was too cowardly to actually do anything about my crush, so he probably thought I was there to watch all the girls. Which I wasn't," he added, darting her a look to make sure she believed him. She kept her expression neutral, and he continued. "So you're running, and you were just so athletic and focused and *beautiful.* I loved to watch you run, okay? I know that's weird but there it is. Normally you were so sweet and laid back, but whenever you played sports you suddenly turned cutthroat, and I liked that." He paused to clear his throat before continuing. "So, anyway, I wasn't thinking about it, and I blurted out, 'She's like an Amazon warrior princess.'

"In my mind, that was a really great compliment because I had just been reading this story about these Amazon women who were supposed to be beautiful and awesome, and that's what I thought when I saw you running. But of course Corby had no idea I meant it in a good way. He thought it was funny. And I tried to explain, I promise I did, but there was this group of football players nearby, and he told them, and then it went viral."

As Vaughn watched Grant try and explain, he suddenly became that fifteen year old boy again. She could see him as if it was yesterday, unsure about how to undo the damage he had done. And then she realized that, not only did she believe him, but that she was actually flattered by his story. He had come to practice every day? Just to watch her? She had seen him there, of course. He had been pretty hard to miss, so tall and handsome with his own crowd of admirers sitting around him, watching him. And all the while they had been watching him, he had been watching her.

"You're quiet," he said at last. "Is that a bad thing? Are you that mad?"

She shook her head. She wasn't angry; she was…what was she? Humbled? Embarrassed? Confused? "Why didn't you just tell me? How could you not have known how much it hurt to have everyone call me that?"

"I didn't know everyone called you that. We both know I'm not the world's most observant person. If I had known…I wouldn't have hurt you, Vaughn. Not for anything." He reached over and picked up her hand, giving it a gentle squeeze. "I'm sorry. It's ten years too late, but I'm sorry about that name. I had no idea something I meant as a compliment would be misconstrued as an insult."

It was surreal, not only that they were here together and he was apologizing, but that Vaughn actually believed him. She squeezed his hand in return. "Thank you for that."

They shared a smile before he returned his eyes to the road. And then they both realized that they were still holding hands. Vaughn's first instinct was to throw it away as if it were poison, but she didn't. She held onto it, staring at it, marveling over the way his large hand dwarfed hers. She turned it over and inspected his palm, tracing her index finger over ridged calluses.

"What are these from?" she asked.

"Rope. Saddles. Fences. Shovels. Wrenches. You name it, pretty much. My work is pretty hands on at the farm." He swallowed hard, his Adam's apple bobbing convulsively, and she could tell he liked her gentle inspection of his hand.

"Want to know a secret, Grant?" she asked, feeling very powerful because such a small touch was having such a profound effect on him.

He nodded, not daring to look at her, and she was glad. She didn't think she could say it if he was looking at her.

"I liked you, too, back then. I had a little obsessive crush of my own."

He smiled and glanced at her. "Really?"

She nodded, smiling in return.

He looked at the road again. "You were good at hiding it. What I remember most from you in high school was a whole lot of exasperation."

"There was that, too," she said, and he laughed.

"Until that one party," he began.

She dropped his hand and turned to look out the window at the upcoming exit. "Can we stop for lunch? I'm starving."

CHAPTER 13

"I thought you said you were starving."

Grant was staring at her through narrowed eyes, as if trying to figure out if she was angry with him. "I was," she said, but after perusing the lackluster menu, nothing seemed suitable. And all of a sudden she was tired of keeping a mental calculation of calories, fat, protein, and the glycemic index in her head. Reluctantly, she decided on a fruit cup, Caesar salad with plain lettuce, and a broiled chicken breast, no seasoning. Grant ordered the chicken and dumplings.

"I hope they're good," he said. "I have a weakness for good chicken and dumplings."

Vaughn did, too. "My mom makes the best." Although, she hadn't made them for Vaughn in years. In fact, she never cooked for Vaughn anymore. Instead, she bought a few bags of things she thought Vaughn might eat and let her prepare them for herself. It must be really sad for a woman who used food as love to have to stand back and not cook for her only daughter.

"You okay?" Grant asked. His hand was lying on the table near hers. His fingers inched closer until they were brushing hers. And suddenly Vaughn was fighting tears, right there in the middle of wherever they were. She shook her head. No, she was most definitely not okay. She was twenty eight and having a total identity crisis. Who was she? What was she doing with her life? Why did she keep such stringent control over herself and her diet when it brought her no joy? A part of her wanted to order a trough of chicken and dumplings and devour it while the other part of her was terrified of ending up as the fat girl once again. What she wanted most of all at this moment, however, was to remove the table from between them, fall into Grant's oh-so-strong arms, and have him tell her everything was going to be okay. And that he liked her.

She had to laugh a little over that irony, and now she really looked crazy as she let out a little maniacal giggle and wiped her brimming eyes. But it was just so funny, in a sad kind of way. She had once been the nice girl, the girl next door, the kind of girl Grant liked. And she hadn't wanted that. She had wanted to be the popular femme fatal who made men swoon. And now she was, and she wanted to go back to the way she had been. But the road back seemed closed, and so she was stuck in this wasteland called "in-between." She wasn't the old Vaughn, and she wasn't the new Vaughn. Who was she?

"Vaughn," Grant said. He sounded pained as he twined his fingers through hers and gave them a squeeze. "Don't cry. Do you want to go?"

She shook her head and took a steadying breath. "No, I'm just… tired, I guess." It was partially true. She hadn't slept much the night before, though neither had he. "How are you feeling? Are you sure you're up for food?"

He shrugged. "It was the only thing that sounded good. It should be safe, don't you think? I mean, they don't call it comfort food for nothing."

Comfort food. That sounded wonderful right now. But, as much as Vaughn wanted to eat something that actually tasted good, she didn't want to bury her feelings in food. "I used to eat when I was sad," she confessed. "I would have a bad day, and then I would go home and drown my sorrows in cookies or ice cream or whatever was on hand. And there was always something on hand. And then I would feel horrible because I knew I couldn't lose weight as long as I did that. Food became a source of shame for me. And then I found this diet, and it works because I keep stringent control over what I eat, calculating every mouthful down to the calorie. It's exhausting, but I like it because I like feeling in control. But eating now is joyless. I can't remember the last time food was pleasurable instead of painful. Maybe when I was a kid, but maybe not. I don't know." She hadn't meant to unload, and now she was embarrassed.

"So when you were eating whatever you wanted, food still wasn't a pleasure," he clarified.

She nodded. "Food and I, we're not friends."

He studied her in silence for a few beats. "You know what you need?"

"A stomach band that keeps me from overeating?"

He frowned when he realized she was serious. "No. Geez, Vaughn, that sounds like a torture device. What you need is permission to let go and eat whatever you want, whenever you want. No rules, no restrictions, no shame."

That sounded heavenly, but, "I can't do that. I'll end up the size of the house. I'll be one of those women the fire department has to use a crane for whenever there's an emergency."

"No you won't," he said confidently. "You just need to get over the initial fear and excitement of eating again, and you'll be okay."

Something like hope began to flutter in Vaughn's—empty—stomach. "Do you really think I could?"

"I know it. You can do anything."

It was uncanny. When he said it, she really believed him. "I guess maybe after this is over I can try to find a therapist who specializes in food," Vaughn mused.

"You could do that. Or we could try an experiment right here, right now."

"What kind of experiment?" Why wasn't she saying no? She should be saying no. He was a farming engineer—she should not be taking food advice from him. But she wanted to. She wanted someone, anyone to tell her how to fix her problems, and food was definitely a problem.

"We're going to be together for the next few days. As long as we're together, I want you to eat whatever you want, whenever you want. Turn off you brain and just eat."

"But," Vaughn started to interrupt, but he squeezed her hand again.

"Just trust me, okay? You are not going to get fat in the short amount of time we're together, and I promise we'll keep active and work off any excess calories. Look at me, do I look fat?" He let go of her hand and sat back so she could make her inspection.

No, he most certainly did not look fat. He looked incredible. "But you're a man," she said. "Everyone knows men have higher metabolic rates."

"That's not the point. The point is that I eat enough for five people, and yet I don't gain weight. I know a thing or two about calorie intake verses output, believe it or not. I'm a science guy, remember. It's just an experiment. What could it hurt?"

"What if I like eating so much that I'm never able to go back to my diet?" Vaughn asked.

"If you want to go back to your diet when this is over, I'm sure you'll be able to. You've been doing it relentlessly for eight years. Think of this as a vacation."

She nodded. "Okay. A vacation. I can do this." She bit her lip. "Though I have no idea what to do. What should I do?"

"Look at the menu again, only this time see what you want to eat and not what you should eat. Close your eyes and try to imagine what might actually taste good."

"I don't need to do that. The chicken and dumplings sound good."

He slipped out of the booth, going to speak to their waitress. He slipped back into the booth. "What about dessert?"

Vaughn's first reaction was panic. "I can't have dessert. I haven't had dessert in eight years."

"Honey, this isn't about what you can't have. This is about what you want. Vacation. Now, what do you want?" He flipped the menu over so she could see the dessert section. "Order one of everything if you like. Or two. The world is your oyster."

"Mmm, oysters sound good right now," she said, smiling when he laughed. She swallowed down her anxiety, trying not to let her hands shake as she made her selection. "I want the chocolate cake. I have a thing for chocolate."

He quirked an eyebrow at her. "Really? I'll have to remember that. May I see?" She handed him the menu and he scanned it. "I'll have the apple pie. I have a thing for pie."

"I'm really good at baking pie," she said, whispering as if confessing a horrible secret.

Grant looked up and smiled at her, beaming in approval. "Somehow I always figured you would be." Under the table, he gave her knee a squeeze and then left his hand there, offering gentle reassurance, which was good because Vaughn felt nervous. She felt the same way she had before the reunion, as if she had to steel herself to meet an old enemy again. But then the food arrived, and some of her anxiety faded away. The little lumps of dough looked innocuous, and so *good.*

"Mmm," Grant said after his first bite and Vaughn paused to admire him. He was being sincere in his appreciation of the dumpling, at least until he realized she wasn't eating. "It's hard to take the first bite, huh?" he guessed.

She nodded, feeling stupid. It was a dumpling, for crying out loud, not an armed assailant. Grant didn't treat her like she was stupid, though. He scooped up a hunk of dumpling from his bowl and held it out to her. "Taste mine," he commanded.

She opened her mouth and waited while he gently deposited the little pouch of dough on her tongue. The first bite was always the best, and this one was especially good because she hadn't tasted anything with flavor in years. Her mouth was exploding with sensation. Suddenly she realized why Shakespeare had written so many sonnets because she could pen a few dozen about this dumpling.

"What do you suppose is in there that makes it taste so good?" Grant asked. "This broth is amazing."

"Umami," Vaughn said when she swallowed.

"What's that? Some special seasoning?"

"No, it's the Japanese word for that indescribable savory sensation. They felt that describing tastes as salty, sweet, bitter, or sour just wasn't enough."

"That's fascinating," he said, and he meant it. "Umami," he repeated. "I'm going to remember that because it's the perfect way to describe something indescribable. Like Worcestershire sauce."

"Exactly," she said approvingly, not noticing until after it was over that she had inadvertently eaten two dumplings. She stared at her bowl, panicked all over again. Her trainer had taught her that mindless eating was the gateway to fat pants.

"Are they as good as your mom's?" Grant asked. His gentle tone alerted her to the fact that he was purposely trying to distract her. She closed her eyes, trying to remember how her mom's had tasted.

"They're pretty close, but nothing tastes as good as your mom's food, right?" She opened her eyes, cutting off a small bite and trying to savor it while she chewed. "Your mom must be a good cook."

"She is, but she doesn't do it often, usually only for holidays and birthdays. One of our presents is that Mom will cook us whatever meal we choose. It's not that she doesn't like to cook, it's just that with so many of us it's practically a full time job. She's very busy in the community, sort of our public representative. She tries to erase any of the damage we've caused over the years by reminding the community that at least one of us is cultured and well-behaved. Although, my sisters-in-law have certainly helped a lot. Everyone loves them." He paused to give her an endearing smile.

"Are you still as close to your brothers now that they're married?" She remembered the Honeywells as a pack, super close and always together.

His smile dimmed slightly. "Oh, you know how it is. People get married and have kids, and things change. We do Monday nights together, just the brothers. But the other nights they're busy with their wives and kids. Not that I don't love my sisters-in-law, nieces, and nephew, because I do."

"You've been lonely," she guessed.

"Yeah, I have." He gave her another smile, and this one was sheepish. "College taught me I don't like being with a bunch of strangers. I like being with the people I'm close to, the people I really care about. But lately they've been busy with other things. Without them, I only have my work, and it's not really challenging enough to hold my interest."

"Surely you must date," she said it as a statement and not a question.

"The last woman I asked on a date ended up being my sister-in-law," he said. "Before that I was interested in someone, but she lived far away and she was obviously in love with someone else, so I did my best to try and help them get together. They're married now."

"Did you have a girlfriend in high school?" she blurted. "You mentioned someone long distance, and there was this rumor floating about you that you had a serious girlfriend, but she lived far away."

He laughed. "No way, people really talked about who I dated? Why would anyone care?"

Because you're beautiful, and no one could believe you weren't *dating someone.* "You must know your family is fascinating to the community. You're our very own celebrities."

He sighed. "Yeah, I guess so. I don't mean to sound whiny, but sometimes that's not fun with everyone watching you, speculating over everything you do."

"If you had said that to me a few years ago, I would have thought you were being whiny. I used to think it would be great to have that kind of status. But now I have it and I sort of wish I could undo it. It's a blessing and a curse, you know? I'm not going to lie—the adulation and the money are great. But the flip side, the lack of privacy and the gossip, they're not so great. In fact, they're pretty miserable."

He nodded. "I guess that's maybe one of the reasons my brothers and I got into so much trouble so people would stop expecting us to be good. Once we had our reputations as mindless goons firmly in place then we were free to be as good as we wanted and we could surprise people instead of disappoint them. Does that make sense?"

"It actually does," Vaughn said, nodding in agreement. They had set the bar low so they were free to live above it. If they had started out being perfect, then everyone would have been perpetually disappointed with them because no one was perfect. This way they had created their own kind of freedom.

"Ready for your cake?" The waitress arrived, smiling. Vaughn looked down in horror, expecting to see that she had cleaned her bowl without realizing it, but except for the first two, her bowl of dumplings remained untouched.

"I'm ready," she said.

"You can finish," Grant said. "I'll wait for my pie until you're done."

"No, I think I'm done," she said, honestly surprised by how easy it was to let the dumplings go. They had been good, and she had enjoyed them, but she didn't feel the gnawing sense to finish. She felt…peaceful.

"Be right back, hon," the waitress said, still smiling as she cleared their plates. And Vaughn was smiling now, too, and so was Grant, though he was almost always smiling.

"You didn't answer my question," Vaughn said. "About the girlfriend in high school."

"Oh, I got distracted. That happens to me a lot. Sorry. No."

"No you didn't have a girlfriend, or no you won't answer?"

"No, I didn't have a girlfriend. I'm not sure how many different ways I can say it until you believe me, Vaughn, but I only had eyes for you. Why would I date some random girl I never saw when you were what I wanted?"

"But you never told me," she said.

He leaned forward as if to reply, but the waitress arrived then with their food. Vaughn was momentarily distracted by the beauty of the three layer chocolate confection. "You want me to feed you the first bite?" Grant asked.

"No, I'm just admiring it for a second. I can do this." She took a small bite, closing her eyes in satisfaction. *Oh, chocolate, how I've missed you,* she thought.

"Good huh?" Grant said. When she opened her eyes, she wondered what her expression must have looked like because he was staring at her, captivated, his own fork held in midair.

Vaughn nodded and held out her fork for him. "Want to taste?"

In answer, he leaned forward and took the proffered bite before loading his fork with a piece of pie and holding it out to her. The pie was delicious. She chewed and swallowed, and then he spoke.

"Do you know what it's like to live with regret every day, Vaughn? Because I do. If I could go back in time and tell you how I felt back then, I would. All this stuff they're saying about us in the media about us being high school sweethearts is torture because it could have been true. We could have been that couple who met when we were five and stayed together ever since. We could have gone to college together and married after. Do you realize we could have been married for six years by now? We could have a baby or two."

Vaughn gulped at that. Married with a baby? Wow.

"You wouldn't have gone to New York or written that book or made the movie. We wouldn't be here right now, running from a brood of pit vipers. There would be no Bernie, no house in L.A. There would be just you and me."

And baby makes three. She couldn't seem to get over the image of them together with a baby, but his other words affected her, too. No New York? She had loved New York. No book? She had written a book that not only was published, but became a bestseller. She never would have lost the weight, never would have met Axle. Hadn't her experiences, for better or worse, made her who she was today? Then again, who was she? And then something else he was trying to tell her began to register. His tone was past tense and "what if." He was telling her it was too late for them. They hadn't gone the high school sweetheart route. They had gone their separate ways. Vaughn had become bitter and famous by writing a barely masked tell-all about him and his family. And he couldn't forgive her for that; she knew it.

"There was once when I tried to tell you," Grant was saying now. "That party after the last football game, I asked you to dance, and then…"

She didn't want to remember what had happened next. "I don't want to talk about the party. I'm ready to go if you're finished." She looked down, not sure what she would find. Had she eaten the cake? She couldn't remember. But, no, she had only taken that one bite. She took another now and set her fork aside.

"Vaughn," Grant said, reaching for her hand, but she stood and slid out of the booth.

"I should go to the ladies' room before we hit the road. I'll meet you outside." She handed him her purse. "Put it on my tab."

He held up his hand, shoving her purse away. "Just go," he said, sounding weary.

For once Vaughn didn't argue, she simply turned and walked away.

CHAPTER 14

Vaughn was quiet—too quiet. Grant knew she was only pretending to sleep in order to avoid talking to him, but that was all right because he wasn't sure what to say. He thought they had been making strides toward resolving whatever issues were between them. Apparently he thought wrong.

It didn't take a genius to figure out the reason she was so upset had something to do with the party, but what? What had the book said about the party? It was near the end, and by the time he reached it, he had already been seething with anger, too much to really take anything in.

He glanced at her, as he had been frequently, taking full advantage of the fact that her eyes were closed. Even though she was only faking sleep, she looked peaceful for once, and not all twisted up in knots as she usually was. He missed the memory of his Vaughn, the one who had always had a ready smile. Apparently, though, her smile had been hiding a whole lot of pain.

He frowned, tightening his grip on the steering wheel. How could he not have known what kids were saying and doing to her back then? She had been so sweet and beautiful; of course she had been a target. Could he really blame her for taking the art of standing up for herself to a whole new level? She hadn't just found a backbone, she had found an acid tongue of her own and learned how to use it. She was a classic victim turned bully.

For a while, he thought she had become everything he despised in a woman—catty, petty, and shallow. But if she was really all of those things would she have stayed up with him all night while he was sick? Would she have confessed her issues with food? When he first saw the way she ate, he had been repulsed, thinking she only cared about maintaining her perfect image. But now he realized it was more about staying in control than staying thin. Vaughn was trying not to become the person she had once been, the person who had been a target for ridicule, and she was doing it the only way she knew how—by rigid self-control. But she was miserable.

The vision of her tasting chocolate for the first time in eight years popped into his head. For a split second, she had looked blissful. When Grant showed up on her doorstep in L.A., she had seemed so hard, but now he realized that had been a façade. Underneath that toughened exterior, Vaughn was fragile. She was vulnerable. She was *sweet.* She might not realize it, but she was the same girl she had always been. If only Grant could figure out a way to show her that being nice didn't mean the same thing as being a victim. If only he could get her to loosen up a little, let her hair down, and have some fun she might realize that she didn't have to be in control of every-thing. Before he could do any of that, though, he had to get her to trust him, and that was going to be an uphill battle, especially with the party hanging between them. How could he fix whatever had made her so upset when he couldn't remember what it was?

After a long time of pretending to be asleep, Vaughn actually fell asleep. She felt confused when the car finally stopped, but her confusion quickly gave way to nausea. She kept her eyes closed, hoping and praying it would pass. Maybe she was simply car sick. She had been so certain that Grant had food poisoning from whatever mystery meat he tasted at the dirty little diner. But what if it hadn't been food poisoning? What if it was a virus and now Vaughn had it?

Or maybe it was the dumplings and cake. She hadn't eaten much of either, but her stomach wasn't used to such rich treats anymore. Whatever the reason, she was feeling sicker and sicker. So sick that she was holding perfectly still. Grant must have thought she was still asleep.

"Vaughn," he whispered. His hand crossed the distance between them, coming to rest just above her knee. He shook her gently and Vaughn almost tossed her cookies all over the car. *I just had this car detailed,* she thought, though the real reason she didn't want to throw up was because she didn't want to do it in front of Grant. She could go inside wherever they were and have a bit of privacy.

To her surprise, when she opened her eyes, she was staring at a hotel.

"I'm exhausted," Grant explained, sounding apologetic. "We've only been driving for eight hours, but I don't think I can make it any more. We're halfway there, though, so that's pretty good. Eight hours tomorrow, and we'll be done."

She wanted to ask where he was taking her, but she couldn't open her mouth. Instead she gave him a tight smile and nodded. He frowned, probably thinking she was still upset with him. Tomorrow she would explain everything. Right now she needed privacy and a commode. Pronto.

He left the car to retrieve their bags. She sat back and sucked oxygen, trying to calm her raging nausea. *Just get inside, just get inside,* she told herself.

Grant opened her door and she sat up, pasting on a smile that was probably closer to a grimace. "You okay?" Grant asked.

She nodded, but she also allowed him to reach up and lift her down. His hands lingered on her waist, a situation which, at any other time, she might have been really happy about. Right now she couldn't stand still. She shrugged out of his embrace and bolted for the bushes, losing her lunch along with her dignity.

Behind her, Grant picked up their bags, loading himself down so she didn't have to carry anything. "Sit there," he commanded, jerking his head toward a small seating area in the lobby. "I'll try to make this quick."

She was still too sick to do anything more than nod. Instead she sank to the couch and bent over, pressing her forehead to her knees in an effort not to black out. She had no idea how long she sat there, but it seemed like forever. At last Grant's hand pressed gently on her back.

"C'mon, Vaughn," he said. He helped her stand and then put his arm around her for support. She looked around, searching for their bags, but a helpful valet was pushing a cart behind them. Apparently they weren't on the ground floor; Vaughn fought a groan as they waited for the elevator. This was not going to go well, but neither would the stairs. Once they were inside the tiny space, she stood close to Grant, resting her full weight on him, her face pressed to his shoulder. He put his arms around her, running his hand soothingly up and down her spine.

"We're only on the third floor," he said, very close to her ear. "We'll be there in a few seconds."

A few seconds felt like an eternity as her stomach rolled and churned, flipping faster with the gravitational pull of the elevator. At last it dinged and the doors opened. Grant helped her down the hallway and slid the card in the door, ushering her inside when the green light came on. The bellhop followed them inside, waiting patiently while Grant helped Vaughn to the bed and then retrieved a tip from his pocket.

The bellhop left and Grant went into the bathroom to retrieve a wet washcloth for Vaughn's forehead. Gingerly, he sat on the bed and pressed the cloth to her face. She swallowed hard, resisting the urge to get sick again. No one enjoyed throwing up, but Vaughn really and truly hated it. It was like surrendering control of her body to a stranger, and it made her feel afraid. Inevitably, though, she was going to get sick again, and she didn't want Grant to be here for that.

"I'll be okay now," she assured him. "Go get settled in your room. You can check on me later."

He smiled. "I am in my room."

"Oh, then I'll go to my room." She tried to sit up, but he pushed her back down.

"I'm in your room, too."

She blinked at him, surprise registering through her misery. "You booked us together?"

"I'm not leaving you alone like this. Plus, it's cheaper." He winked at her. She knew he didn't care about the money, that he was simply staying with her to take care of her.

"But if your family finds out, if people back home find out, they'll think we…" she trailed off, blushing.

"No one is going to find out," he said. "And even if they did, I don't care. I'm not leaving you alone like this. You're not actually worried I'm going to try and take advantage of the situation are you? I mean, I'm lonely, but not that lonely. I like my women flu free, thank you very much."

She smiled as much as she could. "I kind of liked it when you were sick and helpless. You were sweet."

"Aren't I always sweet?" he asked, teasing.

"Yeah, you are," she said seriously. She reached up to rub his cheek, smiling.

"I'm beginning to see what you mean," he said. "Illness must lower the defenses."

"Maybe so." She sighed, squeezing her eyes against another round of nausea. "Grant, I really appreciate what you're trying to do here, but I would feel much more comfortable if you let me do this in private."

"That's what I thought last night, but it turns out I was wrong. It's nice to be taken care of, so forget it, Vaughn, I'm staying."

"Your funeral," she said, then she jumped out of bed, sprinted past him, and dashed to the bathroom.

§

The night was a repeat of the previous night, only in reverse. Vaughn was sick for hours, and Grant stayed with her, gently rubbing her back and bathing her face with the washcloth. He also held her hair until he could locate a fastener, and then he clumsily gathered it behind her face and pinned it in place. He didn't allow her to lie on the floor, though, for which Vaughn was thankful. Bad enough that she had to be sick; to have to sleep on a disgusting hotel bathroom floor would have been adding insult to injury. Instead he waited patiently until she was done each time, and then he carried her to the bed, tucking the sheet under her chin to try and stop her violent trembling.

"You carried me," she said after one such occasion.

"I know," he said. He sounded concerned. Was she hallucinating?

She gave a weak half smile. "No, not now. I mean when I was fat. In ninth grade. I twisted my ankle during gym class, and you carried me to the nurse. I think that was when girls truly started to hate me."

He sat beside her, caressing her overheated forehead with his cool hand. "Oh, I remember that day. I was really hoping it was something serious and they would let me carry you all the way to the hospital. And you weren't fat. You were perfect."

There it was again, the use of the past tense, although Vaughn was too sick to really care. She filed it away for later because the knowledge that Grant only had feelings for her in the past was definitely something worth grieving over.

Her teeth started to chatter as her convulsive trembling increased. She didn't remember Grant shaking this much, but maybe he had been better at controlling it. All she knew was that she was freezing, and she couldn't get warm. "I'm so cold," she murmured. Her eyes snapped open when Grant lifted the covers and crawled in beside her, wrapping her tightly in his warm embrace. He was fully clothed, but still.

"What if I throw up on you?" she whispered.

"Then I'll take a shower," he whispered in return. "I don't think you will, though. You can't possibly have anything left in there. Just go to sleep."

"But…" she started, but he interrupted her.

"Sleep, baby."

Vaughn closed her eyes, sure she would never be able to sleep snuggled up to him as she was, but then his borrowed warmth began to creep over her, and she was asleep before she took her next breath.

$\mathcal{A}$ slight movement beside her alerted Vaughn to two things: 1. Grant was awake, and 2. They were in the exact same position as when she fell asleep, cuddled together like two halves of a clamshell.

"Sorry, did I wake you?" Grant whispered.

"I don't know," Vaughn said, not knowing which of them woke first. "What time is it?"

"Six," he said, and they laughed quietly together. "How are you feeling?" he asked.

"Like I spent a few hours throwing up. Weak, but otherwise good. How about you? Are you fully recovered?"

"Yes. I don't feel weak or queasy at all anymore."

"That's good. That means I'll be back to a hundred percent by tomorrow, too."

"And all you have to do today is sit in the car. That'll give you a good chance to recover," Grant said.

Vaughn thought it absurd that they could be having a normal conversation, as if they weren't snuggled so tightly together their faces were almost touching. She kept her face angled slightly down because she could only imagine what her breath must smell like, and also because she didn't want to risk seeing what might be in his eyes. What if it was regret or, worse, revulsion? He had to be uncomfortable and ready to stop playing the part of her caretaker; only, he made no move to let her go. Instead when he shifted positions, it was merely to draw her slightly closer and touch his sock-clad foot to hers.

"Did you sleep?" she asked. Maybe he had stayed awake all night and he was delirious.

"I fell asleep right after you did, and slept like a rock. I feel great." As if to emphasize that point, he gave her a gentle squeeze. "Did you wake up?"

She shook her head. "It's weird; I'm usually a wild sleeper. I never end up in the same position as I started."

"Maybe you tried to get away, but I wouldn't let you go," Grant suggested. His tone was light with a hint of something more, something that caused Vaughn to finally look up into his eyes. What she saw took her breath away because it wasn't regret or revulsion—it was attraction. And if that's what the look was, then she was pretty sure she returned it because Grant Honeywell in the morning was an amazing sight, all tousled-hair and stubbly cheeks. Not to mention his lips, which were lush and bright red, standing out all the more in his thick morning beard.

"Vaughn," she watched the lips say, and that was all. He said her name and stopped, just looking at her.

"Yes," she prompted after a few silent seconds of staring stupidly at his lips.

"Nothing, just Vaughn. I love your hair, you know that?" He worked a hand free and touched the ends of her long hair.

"You told me once it reminded you of your horse."

He laughed. "I did not."

"You did."

"When did I say something so monumentally stupid? Please tell me it was in kindergarten."

She shook her head. "It was our senior year. It was at the party."

The party. The words seemed to echo and reverberate around the room, even though they had been whispered. "What happened at that party, Vaughn? I don't remember. What is it you think I did to you?" The hand that had gotten free, the same one that had touched her hair, was now cupping her cheek, his thumb caressing her jaw, skimming her bottom lip. How was she supposed to answer when he was doing that? Although maybe she didn't need to answer because right now all she could think was how much she needed to kiss him and to have him kiss her in return.

"Grant," she breathed.

"Hmm," he said, closing his eyes as he continued toying with her mouth.

"Nothing, just Grant," she said, swallowing hard, forgetting everything but his name for the space of a few seconds. Why was she here? Morning breath? Who cared? Not her and certainly not Grant if the way he was now heading toward her mouth was any indication. He tilted closer, intending to replace his fingertips with his lips on hers. Vaughn clutched his shirt, tugging him closer in case he had any ideas about stopping what he was doing, and then the phone rang, startling them both.

"Did you ask for a wake up call?" he asked as his eyes popped open and filled with incredulity.

"Between the throwing up and shivering I was pretty certain I would never wake up again so, no, I didn't." Obviously he hadn't, but she felt compelled to add, "Did you?"

He shook his head. Reaching over her to answer the phone, he inadvertently smashed her into the mattress and then stayed that way because the cord was too short to reach to his side of the bed. But after a few terse comments from Grant, Vaughn stopped caring that she couldn't breathe because she realized the paparazzi had found them. Again.

"How did they know?" Vaughn asked when Grant slammed down the phone.

"I don't know," Grant said. He pressed his hand over his eyes and then swiped it up and down his face, sighing.

"What are we going to do?" she asked.

"What can we do?" he asked. "We're going to have to go down there and walk right through them."

"They'll never let us through. They'll surround us and bombard us with questions and record our responses, and I look like *this*." She grabbed a lock of her lank hair and gave it a rueful tug.

"Geez, Vaughn, we're trapped in a hotel room together, and how you look is your main concern?" he shook his head, rolling his eyes.

Vaughn sat up and closed her eyes against a wave of dizziness. "We don't all wake up looking good, oh ye of the tousled hair and sexy stubble. Pardon me for not wanting to look like I spent the night doing the Technicolor yawn."

"What?" he said.

"The Technicolor yawn, it's a euphemism for, you know, getting sick." She grimaced as the memories from last night came rushing back with a vengeance.

"No, not that, I mean the part about me looking good and being sexy. Say that again." He put his hand behind his head and smiled up at her.

Vaughn resisted the urge to smile, too. Instead she put her hand on her hip. "There's a mob of reporters downstairs, and you're worried about looking good?" she said, mocking his voice and reprimanding tone.

He laughed again as he reached over to pinch her waist. "Why don't you go get cleaned up while I try and figure a way out of this mess, Sundance?"

This time she did smile because of his reference to one of her favorite movies. "Clearly you are mistaken. If anyone in this room is Robert Redford, it's you." He was almost flattered until she continued. "I'm obviously the older and wiser Butch Cassidy while you're the inept and charming newcomer."

"You have five seconds to get to the bathroom before I drop you in the shower with your clothes on," he warned. He was smiling, but she knew him too well to believe he was anything but serious, so she scrambled toward the bathroom and closed the door, stepping back out when she realized she didn't have her clothes or toiletries.

When she reemerged—feeling like a new creation—Grant took his turn in the shower while Vaughn dried her hair and applied makeup. He finished before she did, so he stood behind her, watching in the mirror.

"If I had known it was this fascinating to watch a woman get ready in the morning, I would have opted for a co-ed dorm in college," Grant said.

"That would have gone over well, a six foot eight guy hanging around the women's restroom all morning. I see no potential for disaster with that plan. Nice beard."

Self-consciously, he ran his hand over his face. "Rumor has it that beard stubble is sexy."

Vaughn laughed, delighted he was leaving his face unshaved for her benefit. "The rumor is true." She paused, just looking at him as he looked at her.

"If you're finished, we should probably get out of here."

She snapped to attention, applying a final coat of mascara while he watched. "This isn't going to involve us jumping out of the window and landing in a pool three stories below, is it?"

"I don't think there will be any jumping," he said.

Alerted by his wary tone, she stuffed her makeup in its bag and turned to look at him. "What is it?"

"We're going to leave via the fire exit."

"That doesn't sound so bad," she said.

"We're going to have to leave our bags here."

"No, absolutely not," Vaughn said.

"Vaughn, I know how women are about their luggage, but it's just not possible. We can have them shipped later."

She shook her head. "This isn't about me being vain, Grant, although I appreciate your vote of confidence in my depth. This is about knowing what will happen to our luggage if we leave it behind. They'll go through it, piece by piece. You'll see my underwear and yours on television and the internet. They'll speculate over our choice of lotion and deodorant. We cannot leave them here."

He ran his hand over his face again, sighing as he sat on the bed.

"Maybe I should just go down there and beat the stuffing out of all of them and we can walk out through the front door."

She sat beside him. "I love that idea," she said. "Until the part where you get arrested and sued."

He rested his arm companionably around her shoulders. "Don't be crazy, Vaughn. We'd slip out before I was caught and then go on the lam, turning our adventure into a kind of Bonnie and Clyde thing."

She laid her head on his shoulder. "Maybe we could just hole up here and wait them out. They've got to give up and go away eventually. Meanwhile we could order room service and watch television."

"Sweetheart, I'm not spending any continued length of time with you in a hotel unless we sneak up a preacher to hear our vows."

"Oh, of course I was kidding, I mean, I know you and your family are conservative about that sort of stuff, and obviously you wouldn't want them to think you were just in a hotel with some random woman and…"

He cut her off, ending her awkwardness and misery. "You're not random, and the reason we'd need a preacher has nothing to do with my family and everything to do with the fact that if I were stuck in a hotel with you for any length of time, the last thing I would be thinking about would be room service and television."

He'd certainly caught her by surprise with that announcement. "Oh."

He let go her shoulder and clasped her hand, pulling her up beside him. "Let's go. It's time to activate phase one of the plan."

"What's phase one?"

"Room service."

"No thanks, I'm really not hungry." She pressed her hand to her still-aching stomach. After last night she never wanted to see food again.

"I'm starving, but we're not going to eat it. It's all part of the plan to make them think we're bunking down here." He picked up the phone and ordered a large amount of food and then finished packing while they waited.

A bellhop arrived with their tray, nervously checking over his shoulder to make sure he hadn't been followed.

"Did anyone follow you?" Grant said.

"They tried sir, but I lost them."

Grant and the guy shared a smile, a kind of male camaraderie at having evaded an enemy. "Good job. Now I want you to go back there and tell them you had to wait until Vaughn and I found clothes before we could answer the door."

"Grant!" Vaughn exclaimed, blushing three shades of crimson.

Grant ignored her and continued his instructions to the kid. "Clothes were strewn everywhere, and, as far as you could tell, it looked like we're here for the long haul. But say it like you're trying to keep them from hearing you, you know what I mean?"

"I've got it," the kid said, probably feeling like James Bond, Jr.

Grant gave him a generous tip and sent him on his way before tossing a carton of juice to Vaughn.

"No thanks," she replied, catching the juice and setting it down.

"I had what you have, and believe me when I tell you that drinking some juice will make you feel a whole lot better. Plus you need the energy. We're going to take the long way to the SUV."

Vaughn swallowed, looking at the juice again. "I haven't had juice in…"

"In eight years, I know," Grant said. "I'd like to meet the trainer who made you scared to eat or drink anything. He and I could have a good discussion, I think." His exasperated impatience wasn't helping her anxiety, but then he came over and pulled her into his embrace, hugging her tightly. "It's just juice, Vaughn. A little bit isn't going to hurt you. In fact, it has vitamins. You're on a food vacation, remember? Don't you like juice?"

"I love juice," she said.

"Then drink it because you love it. Or don't drink it because you don't want it. Just don't not drink it because you're afraid of it."

His convoluted grammar confused her, but she got the gist of what he was saying. If she didn't want the juice, then that was okay. But if she didn't want to drink it because she was afraid it would make her fat, then that wasn't okay. "I want the juice," she declared, feeling suddenly empowered. He let her go to open the carton before holding it out for her. She chugged it and tossed the empty carton in the trash can while Grant shoveled a few bites of egg and drank some of the coffee.

"What's next, Jason Bourne?" Vaughn asked.

"In phase two, we make our way outside. With all our bags." He loaded himself down with all the bags.

"I can carry some," she protested.

He shook his head. "You're still too weak."

She plucked a couple of the smaller bags from his fingers. "I'm an Amazon. We don't know the meaning of the word."

He laughed, adding a third bag to her load. "I'm an Amazon, not a pack mule," she muttered, but she kept the bag.

"The fire escape is at the end of this hallway, so we're going to have to sprint to make it there undetected. I'm going to poke my head outside the door, and when I give you the nod, then we're going to make a dash for it. Ready?"

"Ready," Vaughn said.

Grant peered through the peephole before slowly opening the door and sticking his head into the hallway. He nodded once and he and Vaughn took off at a dead sprint, heading for the door at the end of the hall.

They made it and paused to catch their breath. "I forgot how fast you are," he said as he set down all of their luggage.

"What are you doing?" she asked. "Aren't we supposed to be leaving?"

"As soon as we go outside, it's going to trigger the emergency alarm, which will then alert all the photographers. I'm going to disable the alarm so it won't make a sound, and then after we're safely away, I'll call the hotel and tell them to reattach it."

"You can do that? You know how to disable an alarm?"

"Baby, I'm an engineer," he said before turning his back to her as he worked on the alarm.

"I am *so* putting this in a book someday," she mumbled. At that moment, she did feel like the romantic lead in a spy movie. It didn't hurt that Grant happened to be movie-star handsome.

"Done," he said as he pushed open the window. He sat on the ledge, reaching in to pull out their bags one at a time before stowing them on the small landing and then reaching back to help Vaughn. She didn't really need his help, but she appreciated it nonetheless. "Ready for phase three?" he asked.

"Is phase three climbing down?" she asked.

"Sort of. The fire escape doesn't seem to go all the way to the ground. We're going to have to jump, but only a few feet. Good thing you're tall."

"I've been waiting my entire life to hear those words," Vaughn said, and Grant laughed.

They ran down the metal stairs in record time, even loaded down as they were with baggage. When they reached the bottom, Vaughn saw a square opening, leading to a ladder that was still tightly closed. Grant unloaded all his bags once again and studied the ladder. "I'm going to have to jump on it and use the weight of my body to get it to fall," he said. Otherwise the jump was a good fifteen feet. Even if Vaughn dangled and let go, she would still be falling nine feet, something that didn't sound enticing on the best of days, and certainly not when she was still weak post flu.

"I can do it," Vaughn volunteered.

"You're too skinny to be effective," Grant said, probably knowing how much she would enjoy the words.

"You're really scoring a lot of points this morning."

He laughed again. "Wish me luck," he said, but then he didn't stay around to hear her. Instead he grabbed the bottom rung of the ladder and jumped, pulling it down as he descended. Unfortunately, he was going much too fast so that when the ladder reached its limit, Grant continued his momentum and was plunged to the concrete, landing hard on his back.

"Grant," Vaughn yelled before slapping her hands over her mouth.

Grant raised one hand and gave her a thumb's up, but he didn't attempt to get up. Vaughn loaded herself with all of the bags and shimmied through the opening in the metal floor, scurrying down the ladder as fast as she could. She still had to drop the last few feet, which was no easy task with all of their bags, but she made it with only a slight bounce before shaking free of the bags and dropping to kneel beside Grant.

"Are you okay? Are you hurt? Did you break anything?"

He shook his head, still looking a little dazed. "Just knocked the wind out of me. I'm fine." With her assistance, he sat up. Not trusting his assessment, Vaughn ran her hands over his torso, checking for injuries. Grant sat perfectly still, blinking at her owlishly. "You missed a spot," he said when she was finished.

She sat back, tipping her head to study him. "I did?"

He nodded and pointed to his lips.

She leaned in very close, but stopped short of kissing him. "You missed the fact that I don't make the first move," she whispered, causing him to laugh again. He stood shakily to his feet and put down a hand to her, but he didn't try to kiss her. Instead he loaded himself up with the bags once again.

"On to phase four—making it to the car undetected. This is going to be tricky."

And it was. They had to walk a half mile before they could safely cross the street without being seen from the hotel. Then they had to snake their way back to the hotel parking lot, weaving in and out behind buildings. Once they were finally close enough, they had to get down on their hands and knees and crawl to the parking lot, praying no one had staked out their car.

Finally, at last, they were inside the car and safely on their way when Grant spoke. "Now comes phase five, and it's the hardest part."

"What's phase five?" Vaughn asked, turning to see if they were being followed.

Grant glanced at her as he pulled out his phone. "Phase five is when I call my mother and try to explain to her how I spent the night in a hotel with you and nothing happened."

CHAPTER 16

*V*aughn was still laughing when her phone rang. It was Axle.

"Darling, why are you in Idaho?"

"I'm in Idaho?" she asked, darting Grant a questioning look, one he didn't acknowledge.

"According to the television, yes," Axle said. "Darling, I'm worried about you. Are you okay?"

"I'm fine, Ax. We had a little adventure getting away from the Paps this morning, but all is well, and we're on our way."

"On your way to where? Where is he taking you?"

"I don't know." She turned to Grant. "Where are you taking me?"

Once again he didn't answer. He simply pressed his lips together and continued driving.

"He won't say," Vaughn said.

Axle clucked his tongue in disapproval. "This man broke your heart, no, he crushed it, and yet you're with him again. What are you doing?"

"It's not that simple," Vaughn said.

"It really is. You know how it is in this business, Vaughn. You keep your heart from being involved, period. Do I need to list for you the people who haven't done that, the people who have wound up heart-broken and crushed because they were too stupid to keep a cap on their emotions? You know better—do better, because I don't want to have to be the one who picks up the pieces of your shattered heart and tries to put you back together when this ends badly, and we both know it will end badly. There's no such thing as the fairy tale. Don't delude yourself into believing there is. Maybe you should pick up a copy of your book and read it again."

There was no need to reply because Axle hung up on her.

"That didn't sound friendly," Grant said. He sounded like he was the one trying to keep a cap on his emotions, namely anger.

"He's worried about me. Its…you have to understand the world we live in, Grant. Everyone is so fake all the time. Everything is a show. More often than not the line between public persona and private individual becomes indistinguishable. People end up believing their own hype; they end up being a famous movie star all the time, losing sight of who they really are." As she spoke, she realized that she was including herself in that description. Somewhere along the way, she had stopped being Vaughn from Kentucky and started being Vaughn the Gossip Columnist, a cold, social-climbing backstabber who would have sold out her own mother for a story. Perhaps writing her book had been a last-ditch effort at self preservation, a way to get out of her destructive and dissatisfying lifestyle, only she had written the book about someone she knew, someone she actually cared about. Wasn't that worse than when she had been reporting on strangers?

Sensing her negative emotional state, Grant reached over and took her hand, holding it as the miles passed. All of a sudden, Vaughn wanted to cry, and she wasn't sure why. Was it because Grant was being so nice to her when, really, he should hate her? Or was it because Axle had burst the little bubble she had been building, the one that believed she could have it all, the one that told her Grant would forgive her and they would live happily ever after? Maybe it was simply because she had spent much of the previous evening heaving into a toilet in the middle of who-knows-where Idaho, and she still felt miserable.

"Ready to stop for breakfast?" Grant asked.

Vaughn nodded, though she didn't mean it. If there was one thing she wasn't ready to face right now, it was her continuing struggle with food. But she knew he had to be starving after this morning's maneuvers to get away from the paparazzi. She used her phone to find a breakfast café, and they pulled off the highway.

Since it was Saturday, the place was crowded. Vaughn didn't feel like dealing with a crowd, but Grant was undaunted. "That must mean their food is good," he said as he helped her down from the SUV. Once again she found herself glad for his help when she took a step and staggered slightly. She must be weaker than she realized. Either for that reason, or simply because he wanted to, he kept his arm around her as he ushered her into the restaurant.

Despite the large crowd, they didn't have to wait for a table. Vaughn started to pick up a menu, but Grant halted her. "Eat what you want, what really sounds good, and not what you think you should," he reminded her.

She nodded, trying hard to read the menu through different eyes, hungry eyes that enjoyed food. To her surprise, something leapt out at her right away. When the waitress came, Vaughn ordered an over-stuffed omelet with hash browns. Grant ordered the full breakfast with pancakes. Pancakes sounded good to Vaughn, too, but she knew she could content herself with a bite of his, and she smiled as she realized she was actually looking forward to eating.

"That's a pretty smile," Grant said, leaning forward so his elbows rested on the table.

"My emotions have been off the charts all over the place the last few days. I'm sorry."

"Why are you sorry? What's wrong with feeling? I'm not exactly what you'd call repressed in the feelings department. When I feel something, everyone knows it."

"That's true," Vaughn said. Grant had no problem expressing happiness, sadness, anger, or even fear to some degree. It was nice to be with someone real, someone who didn't have to calculate how every emotion was going to play out in front of the people around him. As she watched, Grant's happy smile slipped to something like melancholy.

"What's between you and Bernie?" he asked, his tone serious. "I really want, no, need to know." He bit his lip as he waited for her answer.

Was it possible he was actually jealous of Axle? That was almost laughable, though his expression was so earnest, so worried, that Vaughn couldn't find any amusement. "Friendship."

"That's it? Never a hint of anything more?"

She shook her head. "We've both been too busy building our careers for that. I told you that we're kindred spirits, and that's true. We understand each other, we know where we started from, and that's given us complete trust in each other."

To her dismay, the news didn't make him happy. Instead it made him frown. "It kills me that you've given this guy your complete trust when you won't give it to me."

"I trust you," she insisted.

He shook his head. "Not completely. You still have issues from high school. You still think I did things that hurt you."

He had her there. "It's just hard to reconcile my reality with yours, Grant. Our version of events don't add up. I can only go by what I felt and experienced."

"Then let's talk about it, and I'll explain. You'll see that I had nothing to do with anything that happened to you. And, if I had known what was going on, I would have defended you. I would have protected you."

The prospect of Grant as her protector was enough to make her want to cry again. If she had known he was on her side back then, she could have laughed at whatever people threw at her. Part of what had hurt her so much was thinking he was one of the people doing the laughing. He said that he wasn't, but how could so many events be a coincidence?

Their food arrived and they ate in silence for a few minutes. Even though Vaughn was deep in thought, she couldn't help but enjoy the omelet. She shared a bite with Grant and took a bite of his pancakes, belatedly realizing she had forgotten to ask permission. She smiled sheepishly as she chewed, and he laughed, pushing the plate closer to her reach.

"Tell me something else from high school, another painful event you think I was a part of," Grant commanded.

The party was never far from her mind, but she couldn't bring herself to talk about it. "The last football game of the season, do you remember?"

"I remember that night," he said, his gaze intense as it fastened on her.

"You came down out of the stands and did a bunch of flips, and then I flipped you over my back."

He interrupted her with a laugh. "Oh, that. I couldn't believe you could actually flip me, but you were always so determined, always so intent on proving me wrong."

"I was intent on not flashing my undergarments to the world, but then you flipped me, and everyone saw. And laughed. A lot."

"What?" he asked, clearly confused.

Obviously she was going to have to spell it out for him. "I was wearing a girdle, Grant. That's why I didn't want you to flip me, and when you did, everyone saw. It was a big joke for the rest of the year."

"What?" he repeated. "I don't remember that at all. I remember the flipping, and I remember people laughing, but I thought it was because they were having a good time."

She just looked at him. Was he telling the truth? How could he not have known? "But you touched it. You asked me what it was."

"Vaughn, I may have a sister, but that doesn't mean I have any clue about women's undergarments. I'm sure I thought it was part of your uniform." He shrugged. "I had no idea there was anything unusual about it. In fact, I can't even remember seeing it."

That just wasn't possible. How could something so monumental to her be so meaningless to him, unless he wasn't telling the truth. And if he didn't know the girdle held any significance, then how did that explain what happened later at the party?

"I can see you don't believe me," he said, irritated. "But, for the millionth time, I thought you were perfect. Why would I have cared what you were wearing under your skirt? I probably touched it because I was looking for any excuse to touch you."

Vaughn was becoming irritated now, too. "Pardon me if I find that hard to believe."

He opened his mouth to reply, but they were interrupted by a loud scream. Everyone in the restaurant turned to look at a teenage waitress across the room, but she was looking at them. And pointing. "It's you," she yelled as she stumbled forward. "It's Violet and Grady."

"Uh," Vaughn said, as mortified as she knew Grant must be. "Did you want an autograph or something?" She tried to say it quietly in the hopes that the teenager would calm down, but it didn't much matter. They were now the focus of the entire café.

The girl shook her head and to Vaughn's dismay she looked angry. Grant must have thought the same thing because he picked her up hand and gave it a squeeze. Was he signaling her to run? Before she could decide, the girl spoke again.

"I can't believe you are with him." She jutted a finger at Grant. "I mean, what are you thinking, Violet? That guy like ruined your life. He's handsome, but what about Baxter?"

"Hey, now," Grant said, trying to interrupt, but it did no good because the girl turned her fury on him.

"And you," she added. "Haven't you done enough to her? You made her life a misery in high school. Can't you just leave her alone?"

"I'm not exactly Violet," Vaughn tried to explain. "Those are characters in a book. Baxter doesn't even exist. And he's not Grady." She gave Grant's hand a squeeze. "He and I are old friends."

"I know. You've known him since high school, but that doesn't change what he's done to you. Don't let him fool you, Violet," the girl said. Clearly she wasn't dealing with a full deck of cards.

"It's not like that," Vaughn said.

"Look at you," the girl continued undaunted. "Holding hands with him, after what he did to you at that party."

Grant shifted, sitting up interestedly. "What did I do to her at the party?"

Vaughn shot him a you're-not-helping look, but he ignored her.

"You know what you did," the girl said, her tone scathing. "Shame on you."

Thankfully a person Vaughn could only assume was the manager of the café finally came out to retrieve the waitress. "I'm so sorry," he apologized. "This is my daughter, and she gets really into the books she reads. Please consider your meal on the house. I'm sorry," he added as he dragged his daughter out of sight into the kitchen.

The awkward silence in the restaurant was palpable.

"Finished?" Grant asked. His tone was strained.

Vaughn nodded. Her throat felt so tight that she was sure she would never eat again. He fished some bills from his pocket and threw them on the table before taking Vaughn's hand and practically dragging her out of the restaurant. He opened the door to the SUV and tossed her inside before going around to his side and jumping in. And then he just sat there. He looked as shell shocked as Vaughn felt.

She had to say something, though. She laid her hand on his arm. "Grant, I…" she didn't get much farther than that before he started laughing. He turned to her, laughing so hard that tears began streaming down his cheeks. He tried to speak, but couldn't, so he shook his head, laughing harder. A laugh bubbled out of Vaughn, and then she was laughing as uncontrollably as he was. It was part hilarity, part nervousness, and part disbelief.

"I mean, we're in the middle of *Idaho*," Grant finally said, and they laughed even harder. He bent over the steering wheel, and Vaughn doubled over, too, howling with laughter. At last they were all laughed out, but still they sat, wiping their eyes and staring through the front windshield.

"I'll say this much about your life, Vaughn," Grant said at last as he started the car. "It's not boring."

And that, coming from him, was high praise, indeed.

CHAPTER 17

Somehow, Vaughn slept again. Maybe she was finally making up for all the sleep she had missed since arriving in L.A. All she knew for certain was that they crossed the border into Montana, and then she was out like a light.

"We're here," Grant said and unknown time later.

Vaughn opened her eyes, but the car was still moving. They turned from a gravel road to a dirt road marked "Flying K Ranch."

"You brought me to a dude ranch?" she said, confused. Perhaps he was going to make her take a working vacation as kind of a get-back-to-nature type thing.

"Remember that I told you Ivy married a Yankee? He's a King; he and his brothers own this ranch."

Vaughn wasn't sure how to feel about that for Ivy's sake. Was trading horses for cows a step up or down? Since he had said they were there, Vaughn kept expecting to see a house, but none ever emerged. There were cows, however, and a whole lot of fence. Unlike the Honeywells' property, this fence wasn't pretty and pristine white wood; instead it was miles and miles of wicked-looking barbed wire. Vaughn began to feel slightly claustrophobic, as if she were being led to a prison, which was preposterous considering the vast amount of space around them. They had been driving what felt like forever with no trace of human inhabitants.

"Are you sure this is their road?" she joked to cover her nervousness. What if Ivy took one look at her and told her to buzz off? What if she was as angry as Grant had been about the book?

"No, this isn't their road. This is their driveway." He arched an eyebrow at her, and she whistled appreciatively.

"Can you imagine living somewhere so remote?" she asked.

"Previously my answer would have been no, but after the last couple of days I would say yes."

Vaughn frowned. "I'm sorry it's been so…well, you know."

He smiled. "Vaughn, you always think the worst. I meant it would be nice to find an isolated spot to be with you for a while. Every time we start to have a conversation we're interrupted."

"Oh," she replied, turning to look out the window at more cows and barbed wire. He wanted to be isolated with her? That was interesting and unexpected. Logic told her she had brought so much misery into his life that he should drop her off here in the middle of nowhere and run away, as far and as fast as he could. Her hand tensed on the door as a new horror emerged. "You're not going to leave me here, are you? Like just drop me off with the cows and take off?"

"Vaughn," he said, shaking his head.

Was that a no, or was he simply exasperated that she had stumbled upon his plan? What would she do here in the middle of nowhere with nothing and no one? Surreptitiously she pulled out her phone and looked at it, guessing correctly that there was no signal. Just when she was beginning to feel really anxious, they rounded a bend in the road and several buildings zoomed into view.

The first was a beautiful farmhouse, bigger even than the Honeywell house. It reminded her a little of Southfork from the old *Dallas* soap opera reruns her mother used to watch. There were no giant white pillars, but the size and layout were similar with several wings abutting the main house. Behind it was a modern-looking ranch house and off to the right was an old house that had obviously been refurbished and modernized. In addition to the three houses, there were several large barns and something that looked like a dorm.

"The bunkhouse for the cowboys," Grant explained when he noted the direction of her gaze.

"There are cowboys?" she asked.

He frowned at her interested tone. "Most of them are either married or toothless."

She rolled her eyes. "Easy there. I'm not trolling for a husband. I'm thinking of writing a western for my next book. It would be interesting to meet a few real cowboys." When he started to open the door, she put out a hand, holding him back.

"Is it okay that we're here?" *Does everyone hate me? Am I going to spend the entire visit feeling like the bad guy?*

"It's more than okay. They're dying to meet you."

As if to back up his statement, when Vaughn turned to survey the house again, a whole gaggle of people were standing there, staring toward the truck. She recognized Ivy right away, and her heart sank. Despite the fact that she'd had at least one child, Ivy looked as willowy and beautiful as she always had. Her light blond hair and big blue eyes stood out in contrast to everyone around her. It was probably wrong that a little part of Vaughn had been hoping Ivy had gotten fat and ugly, but that was how she felt. No doubt if Vaughn ever had kids her hips would shift so much that it would trigger an earthquake warning. Life just wasn't fair sometimes.

Vaughn waited nervously in the car until Grant came to retrieve her. Thankfully, he held on to her hand as he led her toward the assembled crowd. Ivy stepped forward first, shifting her baby into Grant's arms as she approached Vaughn. Vaughn shied away from her, not certain if Ivy was about to deck her, but instead she hugged her. Tightly.

"Vaughn, I'm so glad to see you again. How are you?" She backed up a step and smiled. "Stupid question, Ivy," she answered herself. "Of course you're probably exhausted from the drive, and Grant said you were sick. I hope you'll get the chance to recover while you're here. I want to spend some time getting caught up, but you won't be staying with us; you'll have more room in the main house." She turned and held out her hand to one of the men, one who was holding a toddler.

"This is my husband, Coy," Ivy said as the man approached. Vaughn hoped her eyes didn't bug because the guy was gorgeous. He was a totally different type than Grant, more easygoing surfer than cowboy, but still. Whoa. Some of Ivy's bubbling happiness began to make sense. Cows were a definite trade up from horses. The little girl Coy was holding was a mini replica of Ivy, all blue eyes and blond hair, though her hair was a mop of springy curls. A quick look at Coy revealed his hair was also naturally curly.

"Five," the girl yelled before launching herself at Grant. He caught her adeptly, not seeming to find it a problem to juggle two babies

"It's so great to meet you," Coy said, and then he also surprised Vaughn with a hug. "Meet the rest of the family," he said as he let her go. "This is my twin brother, Cameron. We call him Cam. His wife's inside. You have to pry her out of the office with a crowbar. I'm sure you'll meet her later. This is my brother, Cade."

Vaughn tried not to react to the surprising sight of Cade in a wheelchair. Like Coy and Cam, Cade was very nice looking, although his looks were darker, more brooding, even though he smiled and held out his hand.

"His wife, Layla." Layla could only say hello because she was holding two small children, twins by the looks of it.

"Our youngest brother, Josh."

Okay, what was up with the water in Montana? Josh was the prettiest brother of all, his sandy blond hair, royal blue eyes, and deep dimples making him appear like a Ken doll. He also seemed the most shy, hanging back slightly as he tipped his hat and mumbled an inaudible hello.

"His wife, Sam," Coy added. Sam was one of those tiny creatures who made Vaughn feel like a giant in comparison, but she smiled sweetly and offered her hand, juggling a baby of her own to do so.

A tall figure emerged from the house. Vaughn looked up to see a pretty Native American woman descending from the porch, holding a baby. She figured it must be Cam's wife, especially when the baby in her arms reached for him.

"This is PJ," Coy introduced. "She's our, uh…" He broke off, looking at Cam for direction.

"Farrier," Cam said. "And, uh, au pair," he added begrudgingly while everyone else tried not to snicker.

"There you have it," said Coy. "She's his fauxpair." Everyone laughed at that, everyone except Cam, and then Ivy poked Coy in the side.

Obviously Vaughn was missing one of those insider family jokes. "I'll explain it later," Grant assured her in an aside. Another figure emerged from the house, this time a man and—heavens—he was handsome, too.

"There's a crisis in New York. You're going to have to blast her out of there with dynamite today," the man said to Cam who sighed and excused himself to go inside.

"That's Ethan," Coy said. "PJ's husband and Cam and Belle's secretary."

Why were Cam and Belle the only ones with a secretary and nanny? That was odd. But a second later the mystery was cleared up when Cam returned with a woman in tow, and no one had to introduce Vaughn this time. The woman was a legend in literary circles.

She clutched Grant's arm. "You didn't tell me you were related to Belle Landry King," she hissed sotto voce.

He gave her a look like "What's the big deal?" Obviously he didn't understand why Vaughn was now quaking in her boots, but Belle was *the* go-to agent of choice in the publishing business. She represented some of the biggest names in the industry, and she was notorious for negotiating big contracts for her authors. And now she was steaming toward Vaughn, looking as angry as anyone ever had. Vaughn reached for Grant's hand again, clutching it. Was Belle going to tell her she had hated her book? Were she and Grant close? Was she offended because the book was about her family, however distantly related? Vaughn winced, waiting for the verbal blow.

"I don't usually badmouth people in the industry," Belle began, and

Vaughn resisted the urge to take a step back from her roiling anger. "But your agent is incompetent. I could have gotten you twenty percent more. You should have come to me."

"I...I tried. You rejected me."

Belle blinked once before turning to glance at Ethan. "I told you he was reading things behind your back," Ethan said.

"Well, he's fired," Belle said. Turning back to Vaughn, she added. "From now on, and unless you have some objection, I'm representing you. I've seen your movie deal. You were fleeced. Are you working on anything now? Because I could get you an advance that will make your last contract look like minimum wage."

Vaughn wasn't usually at a loss for words, but she had no idea what to say to the small woman standing in front of her. Fortunately, Cam saved her. He strode forward and put his arm around Belle.

"What my wife means to say is welcome to Montana. We're thrilled to have you here. Please make yourself at home. Later, perhaps after you've had a chance to settle in, maybe you two can discuss business."

"Thank you," Vaughn said, still a little confused by the rapid turn of events. The last thing she expected when she arrived here was a new agent. She would need to talk to Axle about this. Her current agent was a friend of his, but Axle was generally a bottom line kind of person. He would most likely urge her to go with Belle, knowing what a boon to her career it would be.

"Oh, by the way, I loved the book," Belle added, smiling now as she turned and went inside.

"She's normal after you get used to her," Grant said. "She's actually very funny."

Vaughn nodded, still feeling a little shell-shocked. The group began to disperse, including Coy, who reached out and took his kids from Grant, until only Ivy remained. "I really loved the book too, Vaughn," Ivy said.

"Ivy," Grant said. "Our family wasn't portrayed so well in that book."

"Yes, but I was," Ivy said. "You really captured what I felt in high school."

"She made you seem like a hapless victim of your overbearing brothers," Grant said.

"Exactly," Ivy said, her tone dry. "I love you, Grant, but my childhood wasn't exactly easy."

"What is it with you two?" Grant asked, getting angrier by the second. "Two of the women I cared about most in the world think I'm some sort of...All I need is for Mom to show up and tell me how horrible I was, and the circle will be complete." He left them, stomping to the back of the vehicle to retrieve their bags.

"I'm sorry," Ivy said. "I should have waited to say something until he was out of earshot. I didn't mean to stir things up between you. It's just such a relief to know that someone else understands what I was going through back then. And it wasn't just my brothers. High school was hard."

Did Vaughn's jaw drop? "High school was hard for you?"

Ivy nodded. "Kids were mean. They thought my life was perfect because I was a Honeywell. They made horrible, snide comments. I had very little self esteem when I came here. Do you know I had never dated anyone until I met Coy?"

"No way," Vaughn blurted. "I mean, I knew it was your brothers made that impossible in high school, but I thought you would break free in college."

Ivy shook her head. "I was too insecure. I met Cam on the internet, came out here to meet him in person, and fell in love with Coy instead."

"Wow," Vaughn said. Ivy had apparently endured some excitement of her own.

Ivy laughed. "You'd die if I told you how much drama goes on out here in the boonies. It's all very *Days of our Lives*. But I'm sure Grant's told you all about it. He had his own share of drama with PJ and Ethan." She could tell from Vaughn's expression that she had no idea what she was talking about. "Great, Ivy, just great," she muttered. "I should go away and stop talking now. Suffice it to say PJ and Ethan are happily married, and they're all friends."

"Grant liked her, but he helped them get together," Vaughn said, remembering what Grant had told her about the last woman he had been interested in.

Ivy nodded. "Come inside and I'll show you to your room." Ivy led her down a hall of the main house and to a suite, complete with its own bathroom. Grant followed them in, dropped Vaughn's bags, and departed without a word.

Vaughn sighed.

"This is my fault. He's angrier at me than he is at you," Ivy said.

"I'm not too sure about that," Vaughn said. He might be irritated with her sister, but in the end it all came back to Vaughn and her book.

"I'll talk to him," Ivy promised. "Freshen up, get comfortable, and make yourself at home. Belle and Cam, Josh and Sam live here, and they're all really laid back when it comes to house stuff. But if you need something you don't see, you can ask any of us."

"Thanks, Ivy," Vaughn said. She paused. "I know you said you liked my book, but I want to reiterate that I never meant to hurt you or any of your family with it. Except maybe Grant, but that's another story. And I always liked you in high school." *Even though I was insanely jealous of your blond perfection.*

"Thanks, Vaughn. I really wasn't offended by the book, although I had trouble seeing Grant as the bad guy. He's only overbearing when he's being protective; otherwise he's a total sweetheart. I hope you guys can sort things out. And, for the record, I liked you, too, even though I was really jealous of you."

"*You* were jealous of *me*?" Vaughn said.

Ivy nodded. "Is that totally ridiculous to admit after all these years? But you were so free and fun. Everyone liked you, and you were athletic and pretty. You were a cheerleader. My brothers wouldn't let me cheer because they said they knew too much of what could happen. At the time, I thought they were protecting me from guys, but after reading your story, I wonder if they were protecting me from other girls. Sounds like it was catty."

"Sometimes. There were good moments, too. I probably didn't play those up very much in the book." Something else to feel guilty about. Why had she written that stupid book? It was like exposing her diary for all the world to see.

"I'll talk to Grant," Ivy said. Smiling, she backed from the room and closed the door.

CHAPTER 18

*I*vy found Grant sitting in the den, arms crossed, staring at the blank television.

"Good show?" she asked.

He turned toward her and made a show of looking behind her. "Are you sure it's safe to be alone in here with me? Maybe you should go get your Yankee to make sure I don't repress you." He turned back toward the television again.

"Okay, I'm sensing you're angry," she said, sitting down beside him.

"Angry? Why would I be angry? Just because my baby sister thinks I'm an ogre, why would that make me angry?"

"I'm going to go out on a limb here and say I'm not the only source of your outrage," Ivy said.

"You're part of it," Grant said, stubbornly refusing to admit he was upset about Vaughn. "Was it really that terrible, Ivy, growing up with us?"

"Sometimes," Ivy said, not wanting to hurt him, but needing to be honest. "It took me a long time to figure out that the reason that no guys wanted anything to do with me wasn't because of me at all, but because they were afraid of you. I thought, well, I thought men found me repulsive."

He stared at her, stunned. "What? You're beautiful, and sweet, and special." He ground his palms into his eye sockets. "What is it with you women and the stupid things you believe? It's like you're looking in a mirror that lies."

"We believe what's easiest to believe about ourselves," Ivy said. "I was horribly insecure. It took me a long time to open up to Coy, to believe he really found me attractive."

"So you ran off and married a Yankee because of me?" he asked, aghast.

She laughed. "Of course not. I married a Yankee because I fell in love. Look, you guys were overprotective, and a lot of the time I hated it, but that was then. This is now. Now I have two daughters, and I can't tell you how much I wish they had five older brothers to watch out for them the way you did for me. There was a flip side to the insecurity coin. I may have resented it at times, but you succeeded in what you set out to do. I arrived on Coy's doorstep innocent and unscathed. When I think of what could have happened to me, all the ways men could have taken advantage of me or hurt me, I'm truly grateful for you and the other four goons. It was a little over the top, but it was love, and I'm thankful for it." She hugged him tightly around the neck. Never able to keep up his anger for long, he gave in and hugged her in return, resting his head on her shoulder.

"I messed up with Vaughn, Ivy, and I don't even know how," he said, finally getting to the heart of what was really bothering him. "I've never been so afraid in my life as I am of losing her again."

"You love her," Ivy said.

"Of course I love her. I've spent most of my life adoring her." He let her go and sat back, staring desolately once again at the dead television.

"Grant, is it really Vaughn you love, or the idea of Vaughn?"

"What's the difference?"

"The difference is that the idea of Vaughn is perfect. The real Vaughn has flaws, namely that she wrote a really scathing book about you."

Vaughn, who had gone in search of Grant, hoping to talk, paused outside the den when she heard voices.

"Ugh, the book," Grant said. "*The Honeybear Chronicles*. What kind of a ridiculous title is that, anyway?"

"I think it's cute," Ivy said.

"You would," Grant said. "Apparently you're both affected with the same kind of crazy." He smiled as she laughed and shoved at his shoulder. "Seriously, though, Ivy. Vaughn's a mess. She's one big ball of anxiety, she's surrounded by people who don't know their head from their foot, and yet she's all alone, she's probably a workaholic, she has an eating disorder, she's bitter, hurt, and damaged."

At that point, Vaughn had heard enough. Silently, she turned and made her way back to her room, closing herself in until it was time for supper. In the den, however, Grant wasn't finished.

"So, no, I don't think she's perfect. But I think underneath all the clutter, she's one of the sweetest, funniest, quirkiest, bravest, and most beautiful women I've ever met. I mean, you should have seen her today as we're running from these Paparazzi. It was magical. I wasn't taking it easy on her, and she was keeping up. Do you know how rare it is to find a woman who can give as good as she gets? No, she's not the Vaughn of my dreams, but she's still my dream girl. Does that make sense?"

Ivy nodded, biting her lip to hold back either a cry or a smile because she couldn't tell which she wanted to do most right then. "That's really sweet, Grant. Have you told her all that?"

"I can't until we clear up the stuff from high school." He dropped his head into his hands and groaned. "I can't believe all the stupid stuff I did when I was seventeen has the potential to ruin my life now. What am I supposed to do when she won't trust me?"

"Teach her to trust you. Be there. Care for her. Build a relationship."

Grant sat up and looked at Ivy. "Hey, you've read the book. What happens at the end, at that party?"

"I don't want to get involved in this any more than I already am, and I think you need to hear it from her. But it's pretty bad, Grant. It's the kind of thing that leaves scars on a woman's heart." He looked so discouraged that she hastened to add, "But I don't think you did what she thought you did. I can't believe it of my big brother." She squeezed his bicep and left him to stew in his uncertainty.

Vaughn and Grant didn't see each other again until supper, which would have been a tense affair if not for the family's affability and interest in Vaughn. They asked gentle questions, either truly curious about her, or trying to cover the horrible silence emanating from Grant. Like everyone else, Vaughn knew silence and Grant weren't exactly two words that often went together. By nature, he was a chatty, happy person. His newfound thoughtfulness was disconcerting.

After supper, Vaughn offered to help clean up. The sisters-in-law didn't take her up on it, but they did keep her in the kitchen, talking for a long time. By the time the night was over, Vaughn had learned each of their stories, and she was fascinated. Ivy had been correct— they'd had a surprising amount of drama for a remote ranch.

Vaughn hoped Grant would appear to say goodnight, but he didn't. She felt the sting of his neglect all the way to her toes, at least until the next morning when he apologetically told her he had gone to his room to read and had promptly fallen asleep. She knew that once he was out, he was out.

The family was once again gathered in the main house for breakfast. Vaughn had the sense that it was something they only did for special occasions, preferring to eat breakfasts in their own house on regular days. It was Sunday, which meant most of them would be going to church, but not Vaughn and Grant; they were avoiding the public eye, especially after the incident in Idaho. They were remote, but not remote enough that no would recognize them, apparently.

Like most people, the family was curious about Hollywood and Vaughn's experiences there. Except Belle who was interested in the technical aspect of movie making as it applied to authors. It was a sort of ping-pong match with Coy and Layla on one side, asking her who she had met and what they were like, and Cam and Belle on the other, asking her how much creative control she actually maintained.

Vaughn was surprised by Cam's interest, but maybe he was the really supportive type who was interested in whatever his wife was interested in.

"Bottom line it for me, Vaughn," he said at one point. "As an author, if you had to do it over again, would you still allow your book to be made into a movie?"

Vaughn had to think about that one for a while. "I think so, but I would make sure that more creative control was written into my contract. If there's a way to do that. Is there a way to do that?" She looked at Belle.

"There's a way to do that," Belle assured her. "There's a way to do that," she repeated again, addressing Cam this time. Cam tapped his cheek, staring off into the distance as if deep in thought.

He really must love movies, Vaughn thought, although he didn't look the type. If not for the plaid flannel shirt and well-worn jeans, he could have passed for a marine with his crew cut, buff physique, and serious demeanor. He and Belle together probably had enough determination to equal an entire platoon of people. She guessed their marriage was probably a constant fight for supremacy, and she also guessed they wouldn't have it any other way. Despite their near-constant bickering, they seemed very happy together. Oddly enough, Vaughn had once wondered about Belle, wondered what type of man she could possibly marry, if any at all. She wouldn't have pictured a cowboy from Montana, but after seeing them together, she realized how well they worked. They were probably the only two people on the planet who could stand up to each other and live to tell the tale.

On the other side of the table were Cade and Layla. They were one of those couples who seemed to have some sort of telepathic connection, always knowing what the other was thinking or needing. Vaughn watched as Layla passed Cade the salt before he could ask for it and then took it away before he was finished.

"Blood pressure," she said.

He rolled his eyes.

"Doctor," she added, and he was subdued.

In the far corner of the table were Sam and Josh, who constantly seemed to be in their own little world. It wasn't that they didn't communicate with the rest of the family, because they did, but they were also having their own conversation at the same time, something about dogs.

Coy and Ivy were like the quintessential quarterback and cheerleader couple—so perfect and peppy you wanted to hate them, but couldn't because they were too genuinely sweet.

It's funny how each couple takes on their own identity, she thought. She chanced a peek at Grant who was studiously ignoring her. Which couple would they be, if they were ever actually a couple? *High school sweethearts.* The thought popped into her head, unwilling to be ignored. Was that how people would view them if they ever got together? Would they be the star-crossed sweethearts, perfect for each other, but separated for ten years?

No, according to him they would be the co-dependant couple as he tried to help her overcome her many, many issues. *Vaughn's a mess.* She couldn't seem to get his words out of her head. Was that really how he saw her? Of course it was because it was true. She was a mess, too much of a mess for Grant or any other man to want to deal with. She should just go off somewhere private, fill a house with cats, and write her bitter diatribes against the world at large. She could be the female version of the Unabomber, except without the bombs of course. She was in the right place for it, too. Maybe she would get a shack in Montana and set up shop. Then she could eat as much as she wanted, and no one would care.

She jumped, startled, when Grant's hand rested on her leg and gave it a squeeze. "What are you thinking about over there?" he whispered.

"Cats," Vaughn replied.

"You like cats?" he asked.

"Not particularly. What are you thinking about?"

"You, Vaughn, always you." He smiled. Her lashes fluttered in surprise. How was she supposed to trust him when he said one thing to his sister and another to her? How was she supposed to reconcile "Vaughn's a mess" with "You, Vaughn, always you?" Still, he was attempting to make peace, and she didn't want to tread on that for the very simple reason that she had missed him last night, terribly. The way he was looking at her made her feel like she had swallowed a live fish that was now flip flopping in her stomach.

The meal was mostly over. Grant slid his arm behind her, resting it on the back of her chair and positioning himself closer. He was so close, in fact, that she barely had to move to whisper in his ear. "You want to know a secret?"

He nodded, eyes sparkling with anticipation.

"I used to write 'Vaughn Honeywell' on my notebooks in high school."

His hand rested on her shoulder, pulling her even closer so his lips brushed her ear. "So did I."

Now the fish in her stomach had turned into a whole school, flipping and squirming, making Vaughn feel almost lightheaded. Grant caught her hand and brushed her knuckles over his lips, rasping her with his stubble. She looked around in embarrassment that turned to surprise when she realized everyone had vacated the kitchen to give them some privacy.

"Want to take this discussion somewhere else?" Grant asked.

Vaughn nodded, mesmerized, and remained mute as he kept her hand and used it to lead her outside.

"Let's walk," Grant suggested.

"Okay," she said. Their clasped hands swung between them and Vaughn occupied herself by taking in some of the scenery she had missed yesterday. Up ahead, a snow-capped mountain sat far-off in the distance. There were trees everywhere, and the sky was crystal blue. "It's chilly here," she commented.

Grant let go her hand and slipped his arm around her, chafing his hand up and down to rub some warmth into her. "Better?" he asked.

She nodded, smiling. They walked on in silence for what felt like a very long time, so long that Vaughn could no longer see the house. She hoped Grant knew how to get back. At last he stopped, turning her to face him. She thought maybe he was going to kiss her, but he spoke instead.

"I want to talk about the party. I want you to tell me what happened."

She looked out over the horizon. "I really don't want to talk about it. Can't we just enjoy the day?"

"No. We need to get this out there, to get it over with so we can move on."

Move on to what? She wanted to ask, but she was a coward.

"How about this," Grant suggested. "How about we have a race. If you win, we don't have to talk about the party today. If I win, we have to talk about it, right here, right now."

"Okay," Vaughn said. Grant had played basketball in school, but he had been a forward and not particularly fast. She had been a runner, and she was fairly certain she could take him. "What's our course?"

"A sprint from that tree to that tree and back again. First one to touch the tree is the winner."

They walked to the tree together, and Grant called it. "Go!" They arrived at the opposing tree at the same time, but when they turned, Grant started to pull slightly ahead. He was going to win, and Vaughn couldn't allow it. Right before they reached the tree, she leapt on his back. While a smaller woman would have simply hopped on for the ride, Vaughn was tall enough that she actually knocked him to the ground. Then, when he was down, she reached over him, tapping her fingertip to the tree.

Grant lay beneath her, quiet and breathing hard for a long minute, and she began to get nervous. Was he injured or was he angry? Neither, as it turned out; he was laughing. At last he rolled over onto his back, holding onto her to keep her in place so that she was sitting on his chest.

"I win," she announced.

"You cheat," he said. He captured both her hands in his, twining their fingers together. "I can't believe you just did that. No, wait, yes I can. You're as competitive now as you were in school."

"I'm an only child. So sue me." She smiled down at him, loving the fact that he wasn't angry with her. Some men couldn't stand to lose to a woman, even something as simple as a friendly race.

"I can't believe you tackled me and brought me down. Do you know how many people have tried to take me out, and how many have succeeded? The answer is a lot, and only my brothers. And now you." He shook his head, pretending to be sad.

"Think of the damage I could have done when I was fat."

"You weren't fat," Grant said. "You were perfect." Her smile faded, and she attempted to slide off him, but he wouldn't allow it. "What? What did I say? No, let me rephrase that: what do you think I said?"

"You don't find me attractive now. You liked me better fat."

He laughed, a loud bark of laughter that scared a nearby bird into flight. "Vaughn, let me be perfectly clear about what is about to come out of my mouth: I think you are the most beautiful woman in the world at any size, okay? I liked you in high school, I like you now. I would probably like you if you were emaciated or a thousand pounds. It's just you, Vaughn. You appeal to me in a way no one else has." He brought her hand to his face, kissing her palm.

"Then why won't you kiss me?" she asked before she lost her nerve.

"You won't like the answer," he said.

"Why not?"

"Because it has to do with the one thing you won't talk about. It has to do with the party."

"You're making that up to get me to talk about it," she accused.

He shook his head. "I'm not, I promise. C'mon, Vaughn, please? Tell me what happened."

Vaughn took a deep breath. She could do this; she had already written it in a book for all the world to see, after all. "It was after the party, the one where I was wearing the girdle. You and I met up, and you asked me to dance."

"I'm with you so far," he said, nodding his head encouragingly.

"You asked me to go into the room with you, the makeout room."

He nodded again, squeezing her hands as the tension built.

"So I did. I waited for you. You whispered my name and shoved something in my hands. It was a stuffed horse, and it was wearing my girdle. I know because then the lights flipped on and everyone was there, laughing. I stood and ran away. I ran all the way home."

Grant didn't say anything for a long minute. "Okay, here's what really happened," he began. "It took me twelve years of school together to get up the courage to ask you to dance that night, not to mention how hard it was to ask you to go to the makeout room. Imagine me, thinking I'm finally, at long last, going to be able to kiss this girl I've had a crush on forever. And then I showed up, and you were gone. You broke my heart, Vaughn."

"That's not funny, Grant," she said, trying to pull her hands free from his.

He wouldn't let them go, though. "I'm not kidding. I'm *not*," he reiterated, his tone sharp enough to make her stop struggling.

"No, it was you who whispered my name, I know it. Who else knew you asked me to meet you there?"

"Anyone within hearing distance. Anyone who saw us dancing and then watched you walk toward the room. Basically everyone at the party. Vaughn look at me." He waited until she looked in his eyes. "Do you really think it was me that night?"

"I don't know," she said, confused. "I don't want it to be you, but I spent so many years believing it was." She took a breath, trying to steady herself. "You said that night has something to do with why you won't kiss me," she prompted.

He smiled. "I should have known you'd remember that." Now it was his turn to look away. "This is embarrassing, but I'm going to own up to something. We've established that I didn't have some mythical long-distance girlfriend in high school. There was also no one in college."

"There was PJ after college," she reminded him.

He waved his hand. "I thought she was pretty for a farrier. That's all there was to it. I never kissed her." He made eye contact again. "I never kissed anyone, Vaughn. That night with you at the party, that was supposed to be my first kiss and it never happened."

The words floated up and hung between them because Vaughn refused to accept them. It just wasn't possible that this beautiful man beneath her had never kissed anyone. He was the antithesis of her; he was perfect. "Don't say that if it's not true, Grant."

"Why would I? It's embarrassing. I'm twenty eight years old, and I've never been on a date, never kissed a woman, never…well, there are a lot of things I've never done." He looked down, staring intently at their combined hands. "This is the part where you run away screaming."

"Or maybe it's the part where I tell you I've never kissed anyone, either," Vaughn whispered.

Grant's eyes snapped back to hers. "What?"

"I didn't date anyone in high school. Or college. Or after. If you think food makes me anxious, you should see me around men." She tried to say it lightly, to make a joke out of it, but Grant wasn't laughing. Instead, he was blinking rapidly and swallowing a whole bunch of times. "Are you having a seizure?" she asked.

"Maybe," he said. At last his blinking returned to normal, as did his swallowing and breathing. Finally, he smiled. "I think we're going to get a do-over, Vaughn."

"I'm a big believer in second chances," Vaughn said.

"Are you, really?" he asked.

"About some things," she said, and now she was the one having trouble swallowing.

He let go of her hand, reaching up to cup her cheek before sliding his fingers gently to the back of her head. He used that hand to urge her forward. Vaughn closed her eyes as she leaned. There was a snuffling sound, and then she was on her back, Grant firmly on top of her.

"Okay, that was odd and aggressive," she said.

"Shh," he warned, and his tone was beyond strained. "Don't say a word, don't make a move. In fact, pretend to be dead."

There was only one reason people pretended to be dead in the wilderness. Against her own volition, Vaughn opened her eyes because she had to see if what she was thinking was true. Unfortunately, it was. There was a grizzly bear less than fifty feet away, and he was ambling right for them, nose to the ground, curious and intent.

Her mouth went dry, and for the first time in her adult life, she was in real danger of losing full bladder control. Immediate panic overwhelmed her. Her first instinct was to throw Grant off her and sprint away. As if reading her mind, he spoke.

"We run, he chases. Our best bet is just to lie still and hope he's merely curious. Best case scenario, he'll sniff us and walk away."

"Worst case scenario?" she whispered.

"Nothing is going to happen to you," he assured her, covering her head protectively with his hands. Did he honestly think she was going to lie there and let him wrestle a grizzly while she played the helpless female role?

"Together, we're over twelve feet tall," she whispered. "Worst case scenario is that we have to try and take him together. What are a grizzly's weak spots?"

"He doesn't have any," Grant whispered. "Stop talking. Play dead."

She should listen to him. She should close her mouth and stop talking, but it was as if she had lost control of her lips. She opened them to say something else when Grant leaned close and kissed her. Whether he truly thought they were going to die and didn't want to do so without kissing her, or he was trying to shut her up, she had no idea. All she knew was that there probably weren't a lot of people who had their first kiss—ever—in full view of an adult grizzly bear.

It was a simple kiss, a gentle press of his lips on hers, but it was sweet and perfect. At any other time, Vaughn probably would have responded by circling his neck and pulling him closer for another. Now she responded by nearly passing out from fear as the edges of her vision began to fade. At least she wouldn't have to do a lot of acting in order to play dead because she was about to be truly unconscious.

And then a gunshot rang out, loud and very nearby. The bear lifted its head from sniffing the ground and Vaughn could swear she saw it frown before turning to amble away.

Behind them, Coy came into view, the rifle aimed at the bear in case it changed its mind. Grant rolled off of Vaughn and covered his eyes with his hand, groaning. Was he about to pass out, too? She sat up and peered down at him as Coy came over, but Grant didn't remove his hand from his eyes.

"Grant." She gently patted his cheek. Had he fainted? "It's okay now. The bear went away."

"He's not afraid of the bear, are you, Number Five?" Coy asked. He nudged Grant's hip with his boot. "He's afraid of what his brothers are going to say when I tell them he was saved by a Yankee."

Vaughn thought maybe Coy was right because Grant groaned again. "Never live this down," she heard him mutter. Coy chuckled. Bending, he laid a rifle in the grass beside them.

"I noticed you left this behind this morning, and I thought I would bring it to you as I once again remind you never to leave home without it. My gut tells me I won't have to remind you anymore," Coy said, beaming. "I'm going to go now. I have phone calls to make. I'll tell One through Four you said hello."

Vaughn sat cross-legged beside Grant while he remained prone on the ground, his hand still over his eyes.

"This morning I was brought down by a woman and saved by my Yankee brother-in-law." He pulled his hand away from his face and smiled up at her. "And it was still the best morning of my life." He sat up, facing her. "I think there's a part of me that's been waiting for you all these years, secretly hoping you would be my first kiss despite how hopeless that seemed. I couldn't make myself pursue anyone else who wasn't you. I wasn't kidding when I said I looked you up after high school.

"I harbored this fantasy where I would find you, go to you, and everything would be what it should have been back when we were kids, that the night of that party would just continue.

"I'm ashamed to say, Vaughn, that I've spent most of my life afraid when it comes to you, and I'm sorry about that. You have no idea how sorry. All these wasted years." He stopped short as if just realizing how long he had been talking without getting a response from her.

The problem was that Vaughn had no idea what to say. Not only was she overwhelmed, but she was conflicted. Maybe she was a little slow on the uptake, but she was only now beginning to comprehend the fact that Grant had spent most of his life harboring a secret crush on her. As of that fact alone wasn't mind-boggling, now she had to re-filter all of her memories of him through that perspective. She needed time to regroup."

Her thoughtful silence must have seemed ominous to Grant because he began to sink from buoyant to grim. "Vaughn, I..."

He didn't get the chance to finish whatever he was going to say because Vaughn leaned forward and kissed him. She mimicked his earlier kiss, pressing her lips gently to his, only she hadn't realized she was going to do it until it was over, so her eyes were open, staring into his. For a second, he looked as stunned as she did, and then he closed his eyes and embraced her, pulling her closer for a different sort of kiss, one that wasn't so prim.

Vaughn couldn't help the stupid little sigh of contentment that escaped as she leaned into him and closed her eyes. Grant must not have thought it was stupid, though, because his lips smiled against hers as he kissed her again.

They would have remained there, kissing like fools, except for the chilling snuffling sound again. The broke apart, turning together to watch the bear step into the opening once more.

"Maybe he's attracted by the sound of kissing," Vaughn suggested.

"I know I am," Grant replied. He stood, picked up the rifle, and fired a shot into the air. The bear harrumphed and retreated back into the forest. Grant put down a hand for Vaughn. "We should probably go before his curiosity overcomes his fear."

"We should go before that happens to us, too," Vaughn said. Grant laughed and they walked home, hand in hand.

CHAPTER 19

Grant and Vaughn passed by the office, intent on reaching the privacy of the den, when Belle's voice called out.

"Vaughn, can I talk to you for a minute, please?"

Vaughn poked her head in, surprised to see Belle. She thought everyone was at church.

"Sunshine has a fever," Belle explained. "Nursing is the only thing that makes her feel better." One half of her was discreetly covered by a blanket. Vaughn wasn't sure which was most surprising, that Belle was nursing, or that she had named her daughter *Sunshine.*

"Let me give you a little piece of advice, Vaughn," Belle said. "Never make a bet with your husband over naming rights for your future children because inevitably you will lose, and then your stoic, rational husband will suddenly turn into a hippie and decide he loves the name Sunshine."

Vaughn laughed as she took the seat across from Belle.

"I wanted to apologize for yesterday," Belle continued. "I realize I may have seemed a bit, uh, off my nut as my husband would say. Believe it or not I'm supposed to be on vacation, but I have a new secretary in New York, and everything is melting down. It's hard to be in two places at once. And now I've unloaded on you out of the blue. Sorry."

"It's really okay," Vaughn said. "It's sort of nice to know I'm not the only one who has been dealing with stress lately."

"I used to thrive on it. I was one of those people who thought nothing could be more satisfying than my career. And then I got married, and Sunshine came along, and it's amazing how my priorities change. Now I value my free time with my family more than anything else, even my job. But, speaking of my job, I wanted to touch base with you about representation. Have you had a chance to think about it?"

"Not really, but it's kind of a no brainer. You're the best in the business, and I'm not just saying that to suck up."

"Oh, I know; I really am the best," Belle said, smiling. "I still sense some hesitation, though."

"I need to talk to my publicist. My current agent is a friend of his, and I want to give him the heads up before we make anything official. It might have to wait until I get home, though. My phone doesn't work here."

"Use our phone, if you want." She indicated the desk behind her. "In fact, you can use it now. I think baby finally fell asleep, so I'm going to go put her down and take a nap. Don't tell my husband I'm napping, though, or he'll insist on taking me to the hospital. I'm usually not much of a nap taker. Today it sounds heavenly." She smiled and excused herself from the room.

Vaughn stared at the phone, feeling unaccountably nervous about calling Axle. So much had changed in the last few days. Would he be able to tell? Axle was her closest friend, and she didn't keep secrets from him, but this felt different. She didn't want to tell him about Grant. Telling him about Belle, though, was a different story. It was work related, something Axle could always wrap his mind around.

She dialed, drumming her fingers on the desk as she waited for him to answer.

"Axle Brandt."

It took her a second to remember that he wasn't seeing her normal caller ID, and had no idea who was phoning. "Ax, it's me, Vaughn."

"Darling, where are you? Do you know how worried I've been? My phone has been ringing off the hook with questions about you, and I have no answers to give. It's like you just dropped off the radar. Where are you?"

"Montana."

There was a pause for a few beats as he tried to figure out if she was serious. "Montana? What's in Montana?"

"Belle. Landry. King."

Axle sucked in a breath. "You're kidding. You met her? What did she say? Is she interested?"

"She's interested. She asked to represent me, but I wanted to check with you before I let Larry go. I know he's a friend of yours."

"Darling, how many times do I have to tell you that friendship means nothing in business? Of course you're going to sign with Belle. I'll prepare a press release immediately. Are you coming home now?"

Now it was Vaughn's turn to pause. "Um, not for a little while. Funny story, Belle is actually Grant's sister's sister-in-law. We're at their ranch. Things are going well."

Axle knew her well enough to read between the lines. "Don't tell me you've fallen into his trap again, Vaughn."

"It's not a trap, Ax. It's kind of amazing."

Axle blew out a breath. "He's playing you, Vaughn. I can see it; why can't you?"

"He's not."

"He is. You don't know what's been happening since you've been gone."

"What's been happening?" she asked, wary now.

"It's not information I'm willing to impart over the phone. I'm coming there."

Vaughn was certain she'd heard him wrong? "Where?"

"There. Nowherseville, Montana. I'm going to catch a flight. How do I get there?"

"I have no idea."

"Don't play coy, Vaughn. There's nothing you can say to stop me from coming. You might not realize it, but you need me. Plus, I want to meet Belle. I have some other clients I'd like her to sign."

Vaughn relaxed. If Axle was coming for business, that made much more sense. "I'm not playing coy, Ax. They don't have an address."

"What do you mean they don't have an address? Everyone has an address. How do they get their mail?"

"They go to the post office an hour away and pick it up. Seriously, their road doesn't have a name. The town isn't on any map. It's spooky, but also kind of nice."

Axle made a sound that might have either been laughter or gagging. "Okay, now I'm definitely worried about you. Just tell me the fastest way to get there."

"I don't know. I was asleep. All I know is that Yellowstone is a few hours away."

"Yellowstone is a few hours away from everywhere in Montana."

A shadow fell outside the room. Vaughn looked up expecting to see Grant, but it was one of the King brothers. "Josh," Vaughn called.

He poked his head around the corner.

"Can you tell my friend how to get here from L.A?"

Josh laughed until she held the phone out to him. "Oh, you were serious? Okay." He took the phone. "Do you have a large piece of paper and a pen with a lot of ink? Because this is going to take a while."

Vaughn sat back and listened as Josh gave Axle directions from the nearest airport, which was three hours away. When it was over, she said goodbye to Axle who sounded distracted, as if he were already mentally planning his trip.

"Don't get any more attached until I get there, Vaughn," he warned before they disconnected. "I don't trust him. He's playing some sort of game, and I'm going to prove it."

Vaughn wasn't sure she could get any more attached than she already was, so she simply said goodbye without making any promises. When she hung up, Grant was standing in the doorway.

"Everyone is home from church," he said, smiling as he propped one shoulder against the doorframe. He was so large and sturdy is looked like he was the one responsible for holding up the wall and not the other way around. "I think the possibility of quiet time alone together has ended."

"Axle's coming tomorrow."

"You win; your news is worse."

Vaughn laughed. "You'll like him once you get to know him."

"See, that's the tricky part of that statement, Vaughn. I don't want to get to know him. And, maybe it's selfish, but I don't want him to come here. He's had you all to himself all these years. It's my turn now."

"Possessive much?"

"Starting now? All the time, every minute." He came into the office and closed the door. Vaughn's heartbeat thudded louder and louder as he stalked toward her. "I've been doing a lot of thinking the last few days. It's no secret I have a lot of regrets where you're concerned, but the thing I regret the most is my own fear. Why was I so afraid to pursue you, to tell you exactly what I was feeling? So I'm not going to do that anymore. From now on, consider yourself pursued." He stopped in front of her and leaned down, resting his hands on the chair, trapping her with his body. "Oh, and one more thing. I love you." He didn't wait for her to reply, which was good considering he'd shocked her speechless. Instead he leaned in and did what she had recently discovered he did best—he kissed her.

CHAPTER 20

Vaughn woke early the next day after she surprised everyone, including herself, by volunteering to make breakfast. She had no idea where the sudden and overwhelming urge to bake had come from. She had purged that particular hobby when she went on a diet and hadn't looked back, preferring instead to skip breakfast on most days.

But now she stood alone and barely alert in the King's massive kitchen, searching their cupboards for flour and yeast. At least she was alone until Grant came up behind her, wrapping her in his arms as he pressed his face to her neck.

"Is it six?" she asked.

"No. I woke early. I think this is the only chance I'll have to be alone with you until we leave. Who knew a ranch in the middle of nowhere could be so crowded?"

She leaned against him, enjoying the warmth in the chilly kitchen. "I should get started on these rolls or people are going to be suspicious when they wake up."

"Can I help you?"

"Just sit there and look pretty," she said, stepping out of his embrace.

He sat at the kitchen table and smiled. "Done and done."

She wasn't sure she would be able to work under his intense scrutiny, but once she started to combine ingredients, it all came back to her. By the time the family trundled into the kitchen, the rolls were ready to come out of the oven. Vaughn had just finished icing them when there was a knock at the door.

"That must be Bernie," Grant said, sounding less than thrilled.

"He must have traveled all night," Vaughn said.

Cam answered the door and returned to the kitchen, followed by Axle who stopped short in the entryway and stared at the sight of Vaughn, covered in flour and holding a bowl of icing.

"What are you doing?" His tone was so accusing he might have caught her robbing a bank. "You're eating *sugar?* You never eat sugar."

"Technically I haven't eaten anything yet. I was baking," Vaughn replied.

"You bake?" he asked, staring at her aghast.

"Yes," Vaughn answered, her voice small and uncertain.

"I happen to like it that she bakes," Grant said.

"You would," Axle answered, scowling.

"Oh, good, I made it in time for the show," Coy said, passing Axle as he scooted into the room. His arrival broke up some of the horrible tension in the room as everyone chuckled nervously and shifted aside to make room for him. Cam ushered Axle into the room and make the introductions.

"My wife will be here in a minute once the smell of cinnamon rolls wafts down the hallway. She's not what you'd call a morning person," he said.

Axle sat between Coy and Josh, darting angry glances at Grant whenever he had the chance. Grant returned his looks with interest until Vaughn set the rolls in the center of the table, shifting attention to breakfast.

"Those look amazing, Vaughn," Sam said. She didn't speak very often, but when she did it was usually something sweet or kind. "All of us share a weakness for cinnamon rolls."

"So do I," Vaughn said, feeling a tremor of anxiety. The possibility of being fat was never far from her mind. "If writing didn't work out, I was planning to go to culinary school and be a pastry chef."

"I didn't know that," Grant said, smiling.

"Neither did I," Axle said, frowning.

"I think there's a lot about Vaughn you don't know," Grant said.

"Oh, that's right. You're the Vaughn expert in the room," Axle said.

Vaughn cleared her throat and stood to cut the rolls, serving Grant and Axle first in hopes of shutting them up. She was mortified by the attention, and more than a little confused. Grant was jealous of Axle, but Axle was acting jealous, too, which was odd. They had never had that type of relationship before, always keeping things friendly or professional.

The King family tried to keep casual conversation afloat during breakfast, but it repeatedly fell flat due to the heavy tension in the room. Despite her anxiety over what was happening between Grant and Axle, Vaughn felt oddly at peace. Why had she stayed away from baking for so long when it was one of her favorite pastimes? It had been a pleasant activity since her mother used to sit her on the counter and roll dough for pies or noodles. How had she forsaken something that was so much a part of her? She didn't want to let it go again, no matter what happened with her weight.

She had the feeling weight would always be a struggle for her. Past experience told her if she started to eat again, she would gain weight. But maybe she didn't have to gain as much as before. Maybe she could find a happy medium between thick and thin, between starvation and eating for pleasure. She could bake for the people she loved without turning into a shapeless blob herself, couldn't she? Lots of women did.

The sound of forks scraping plates alerted her to the fact that breakfast was finished. "That was delicious, sweetheart," Grant commented with a smile. The "sweetheart" was one of those endearments he used on most females of the species, but Axle didn't know that. His fork clattered onto his plate and he pushed back slightly from the table.

"I've had all I can stand of this. He's using you, lying to you again, and you're falling for it, Vaughn." He stared at her, waiting for her response.

"Ax, can we maybe talk about this later?" Vaughn said, very aware of the Kings awkwardly listening in.

"I don't think this can wait. I wasn't sure if there would be internet access here, so I printed something to show you." He reached inside his jacket and pulled out a piece of paper, sliding it across the table for Vaughn's inspection. Grant peered over her shoulder so he could read it, too.

As if by magic, the room cleared, leaving only Grant, Axle, and Vaughn alone in the vast kitchen.

There were pictures of Vaughn and Grant from high school strewn throughout a story titled, "My Turn, by Grant Honeywell." Vaughn merely skimmed, but the article was scathing and riddled with private details from Vaughn's childhood and adolescence, embarrassing details. She looked at him as he looked at her.

"Vaughn, I didn't write this," he said, his tone urgent. "You know I didn't write this."

Vaughn didn't respond, she simply kept staring at him, thinking how it was like high school all over again. Apparently the silence was too much for Axle because he was the one who broke it.

"Of course he wrote it, Vaughn. Who else would know all these things about you?"

"Why would you write this? How could you do this to me?" Vaughn said, but her gaze moved accusingly from Grant to Axle.

His jaw dropped in astonishment. "Darling, what are you talking about? Of course I didn't write this. He wrote it."

Vaughn shook her head. "No. Grant wouldn't do this to me, and you're the only other person who knows this much about me. Please, Axle, don't make it worse by lying. Tell me why. Is this somehow supposed to help my career?" She was on the verge of tears and that, more than anything she had said, caused him to tell the truth.

"Why do you think I did it, Vaughn?" For the first time in years, his suave British accent was gone and he was one again Bernie from New York. "I was being what I thought you wanted me to be. I was being

Baxter." Baxter, the fictional love interest she had created in the *Honeybear Chronicles*.

"Bernie, Baxter isn't real," she said.

"He could be. He could be me. What we have together is special; I know it. We came from the same place. We started out in this business together. We work amazingly well together. You have to know I'm in love with you. I have been from the beginning."

She tried not to let her shock show. She knew he cared about her because he took more time with her than he did his other clients, but she had no idea his interest was anything more than friendship. "Ax, you and I have had some fun together. We do work well together, and you've been my best friend for a long time now. But we're not from the same place." She pointed to Grant. "*We're* from the same place. The Vaughn you know isn't real and, frankly, she's not a very nice person. The Vaughn Grant knows, that's the real me, and she's the person I like. You and I, we'll never be anything more than friends. I'm sorry, but I'm in love with him, Ax, the real deal impossible fairytale whole shebang."

They sat in awkward silence while Axle hung his head, defeated. At least he was defeated until Belle poked her head in the kitchen. "Axle Brandt, I've heard about you. If now's a good time, I would love to talk business."

The transformation was astounding. He sat up and gave her his best million dollar smile. Standing, he breezed toward the door, looking like a whole new person. Before he left the kitchen completely, he paused and addressed Vaughn without turning around. "Am I still your publicist?"

"If you still want to be," Vaughn said. She really wasn't sure if he still wanted the job.

He nodded once. "Wait until the media hears Violet and Grady are back together. This is going to be huge. If you could time your wedding for the release of the movie, I could guarantee you a box office win." He turned then and gave her a smile, the fake one he reserved for his clients. "Darling," he added. He winked, and then he followed Belle down the hall to her office.

Vaughn and Grant turned to look at each other, not knowing where to begin. "So, you love me," Grant said at last.

Vaughn nodded.

"It's about time," Grant said.

Vaughn laughed. She leaned forward and clasped her arms around his neck. "So, about my book. Are you still going to sue me?"

He settled his arms around her waist. "Maybe. Then again, with some persuasion, I could change my mind."

"I think I know how to change your mind." She traced his lips with her index finger.

"Yeah?" he said, and his voice cracked.

She nodded. "I could write another book."

He blinked at her, trying to follow her disappointing logic. "Another book?"

She nodded. "Being here, learning what goes on at a ranch, it's given me an idea for a whole series. I'm going to write about the King brothers. I think I'll start with Cade and Layla because their story involves both wheelchairs and guns. I was thinking of calling it *Cowboy Down,* but that's sort of cheesy. I'll work on it.

"Of course, after I finish Ivy and Coy's story, everyone is going to be wondering about her five older brothers. Are they for real? And then I'll have to do a series about the Honeywells.

"And that leads us back full circle because I'm going to finish with our book. Grady and Violet are going to get together after a long separation. Everyone will learn that all the stuff that happened to Violet in high school was one big misunderstanding. They'll fall in love, and they'll live happily ever after. What do you think?"

"I think it's missing something," Grant said.

"What?" Vaughn asked.

"Revenge," Grant said. "Readers are going to want to see those horrible Paparazzi get their comeuppance."

"I don't think readers will care one way or the other," Vaughn said.

"This reader cares," Grant said. "And I have a really good idea."

"I love it already," Vaughn said, and she did because he had that look in his eye, the one that told her a Honeywell scheme was brewing, and it was going to be epic.

The next day, the four Honeywells who remained in Kentucky flew to L.A, their wives in tow. People who didn't know the brothers couldn't tell them apart, a fact they used to their advantage. It took the exhausted Paparazzi an entire week to figure out that they hadn't been photographing Grant cheating on Vaughn with four different women at various locations across the city at all hours of the day and night. Instead they had been taking pictures of his brothers and their wives on vacation, pictures that were set up by an anonymous caller with a hot tip, a caller with a suspiciously fake British accent.

Far away in Montana, the real Grant and Vaughn were peacefully beginning their happily ever after.

Thank you for reading *Wild and Free,* the final book in the Honeywells of Kentucky series. For more books, please check out my website at www.vanessagraybartal.com

www.ingramcontent.com/pod-product-compliance
Lightning Source LLC
Chambersburg PA
CBHW021151190726
48288CB00008B/2926